FURIOUS CLAWS

NEW YORK PARANORMAL POLICE DEPARTMENT: BOOK FOUR

JOHN P. LOGSDON

BEN ZACKHEIM

D1607577

CRIMSON MYTH
PRESS

Published by: Crimson Myth Press (www.CrimsonMyth.com)

Cover art: Audrey Logsdon (www.AudreyLogsdon.com)

Thanks to TEAM ASS!
Advanced Story Squad

This is the first line of readers of the series. Their job is to help us keep things in check and also to make sure we're not doing anything way off base in the various story locations!

(listed in alphabetical order by first name)

Anne Morando
Audrey Cienki
Bennah Phelps
Bethany Olsen
Carolyn Fielding
Dana Arms Audette
Debbie Tily
Hal Bass
Jan Gray
Jim Stoltz
John Debnam
Julie Peckett
Karen Hollyhead
Kathleen Portig
Kevin Frost
Larry Diaz Tushman
LeAnne Benson
Mary Letton
Megan McBrien
Mike Slaan Helas

Nat Fallon

Penny Campbell-Myhill

Penny Noble

Rob Hill

Sandee Lloyd

Sara Mason Branson

Scott Reid

Sharon Harradine

Terri Adkisson

Thanks to Team DAMN
Demented And Magnificently Naughty

This crew is the second line of readers who get the final draft of the story, report any issues they find, and do their best to inflate my fragile ego.

(listed in alphabetical order by first name)

Alisia Soles, Amorette Holmes, Barbara Henninger, Barry Johnson, Chris Christman II, Cindy Deporter, Debbie Lindsey, Emma Porter, Jacky Oxley, Janine Corcoran, Joshua Dalton, Juli Nash, Lesley Sharp, Leslie Watts, Lisa Camden Cripe, Malcolm Robertson, Melissa Parsons, Michael Geringer, Michelle Reopel, Scott Ackermann, Susanne Ford, Travis Sleeper, Zak Klepek.

CHAPTER 1

"*Y*ou want dinner?" Mrs. Yee asked me from behind the store's counter. Her heavy accent always made it tough for me to understand her, but she was a genius at cleaning blood stains out of leather. And she was sweet. I always gave her my dry cleaning business.

"Excuse me?" I asked her over my shoulder. I'd been halfway out the door when she shot me the question.

"Dinner!" she yelled enthusiastically. "You want dinner? Free dinner!" She pointed to a slip of paper between her fingers with a big smile. I snatched it and puzzled over it for a second.

Dinner? 347-555-0900

"From your pocket," Mrs. Yee said with great joy. "Secret admirer!"

I studied the handwriting. No name, but the author had pushed down really hard on the pen. The tip went through the paper on the dotted "i" in "Dinner?". Whoever wrote it was nervous as hell. How sweet.

I folded the thing up, smiled and nodded at Mrs. Yee, thanked the gods that Max wasn't with me, and headed back to PPD to do some digging.

Sure, New York City was falling under the shadow of a new, invigorated goblin mob with half-tiger, half-goblin soldiers running around. Every PPD officer was exhausted from the long hours and the stress, but I needed a break from the weight of the city on my shoulders.

A little mystery to solve was just the medicine my weary shoulders needed.

Any other Paranormal Police Department would have an AI to leverage in cases like this, but I couldn't ask Sue, the PPD AI, about the handwriting. He'd let everyone in on my secret before I could finish a sentence. The fucking robot hated me from day one, which was fine with me because I hated him too.

So, I did a little walk around HQ. I checked the handwriting on the desks of the most likely officers. No matches.

I was about ten minutes into my adventure when it occurred to me who the culprit could be.

My heart did a little hop. Detective Holmes?

The tall, handsome, somewhat grumpy NYPD detective had joined us on our last little adventure in Central Park. We'd stood close together enough times for him to slide the paper in my pocket.

"Hey, Max," I said over our connection.

"Busy!" he yelled back with that sharp tone that could cut a fruit cake.

I knew I was asking for it if I kept talking, but the

curiosity was going to mess with my concentration unless I solved this little mystery. *"Quick question."*

"Busy!" he yelled with a sharp tone that could now cut a diamond.

I threw my hands up in the air, annoyed. *"Fuck, Max! I just want to know what your last case with Holmes was!"* Some officers smirked at me. They could always tell when I was arguing with Max in my head.

Max paused. I didn't like that pause. At all. He'd put two-and-two together. I should have known a question like that, out-of-the-blue, would set off his pixie alarms. Pixies always go straight for the most inconvenient, uncomfortable, unwanted conclusion.

"Chase bank robbery last June, I think," he muttered. His curiosity was butting Mr. Grumpy Pants out of the way for the moment. *"Mage had too many shrooms and turned the safe door into a waterfall of orange juice."*

"That must have been tough to explain away."

"No one gave a shit. Just another day in New York. Why do you ask, Black?"

"Just want to know more about the people I work with," I said. It was a lie, but it was also the truth. I always did my due diligence. Max knew it too.

"File's in my office," he said, back to nasty mode. *"Now let me get back to business, wouldya?"*

"As long as you don't tell me what that business is, yeah."

"Let's just say it's tough to find a clean broom handle around here."

"Oh, Jesus Christ, Max!" I yelled out loud. Surround sound chuckles rained down on me. *"I'd like to keep my breakfast down if it's all right with you."*

Some people wear their hearts on their sleeves. Max wore his dark, twisted soul in his voice. So I didn't have to be with him to know when he muttered, *"Whatever,"* that he'd shrugged.

Asshole.

The short walk to his office was as creepy as ever. I took the clangy steps, with their loud echoes of doom that filled the stairwell. I yanked the rickety door open and jogged (okay sprinted) across the haunted basketball court. Something was off about that place.

My heart raced as I flipped through the folders in his top filing cabinet. I wanted to get out of that office as fast as I could. Actually, I was surprised Max even let me in without being present. He was hyper-secretive about that place. Maybe he was starting to trust me more. And maybe he was too into whatever he was currently doing to care. That sent another shiver down my spine.

I found the June case files and looked for hand-written notes, copies, warrants, and the like.

Bingo.

I pulled a copy of Detective Holmes' warrant request out of the folder. I scanned the page quickly. In fact, I had to slow down to make sure I didn't miss anything in the dense form. I found a single line of his handwriting where he'd crossed out a typewritten "Sgt. Holmes" and corrected it with "Detective Holmes, Precinct 76."

The "D" and "n" in "Dinner?" was a match.

Good enough for me.

CHAPTER 2

I'd rather feel flesh tear under the tips of my claws than go on a date.

It's not like I wasn't interested in Detective Holmes. He was a good guy. Smart, potentially nice, handsome as hell, but dating had never come easily for me. I'd tried it in The Zoo a couple of times. One guy was a sweetie, but he was one of the last of the gryphons. They were depressing even before they were on the edge of extinction. The date went well enough. He was charming and funny in a dark way. By the time we were eating our dinner though, I'd given up all hope. He tried to recover by comforting me, but I doubt anyone in the cafeteria could hear him over my heaving sobs.

The other date was with my friend, and last male weretiger on the planet, Mike. It was a fake date, meant to make an albino werewolf jealous. I had such a crush on that guy. Alex Cross was his name. Mike took me to The Zoo's cafeteria and set up an entire corner of the room to look like a romantic Italian restaurant. Red and white checkered tablecloth, candlelight, wine glasses for our grape juice. The Zoo's cook served meatloaf that night so the decor didn't match the meal, but it was sweet. I actually had a good time. And Alex did get jealous.

He got jealous of *me*.

He and Mike dated for a year.

Sure, I could have just called the phone number on the note from the very beginning. But where's the fun in that? I liked Holmes' style. Laying down a little mystery for me to solve was the perfect opening line.

I went to Max's desk and dialed the number.

"What the hell is it now, Max?" Holmes asked. Such a New Yorker.

"I like Italian food," I said quickly. I might have smirked just a little. Game on.

The pause lasted an impressive one point five seconds as he recognized my voice, realized what I was saying, and answered. "I know the perfect place. Tonight at 10 p.m.?"

"10 p.m.?" I asked, dropping into the only human-sized chair in the room. "You a vampire, Detective Holmes?"

"Nope, just NYPD."

I laughed and spun my chair in circles. "10 p.m. sounds good. The PPD bosses are throwing a ball to boost morale. We can head there after."

"You dance?"

"I love to dance. I love to whisper about other people dancing just as much."

"Sounds like a dream date."

"It's not a date until it goes well," I said as I kicked the file cabinet shut with a high kick from the spinning chair.

"This is a good start."

"It'll do. Let's see if you can keep it up. Where are we going?"

He gave me an address in the Lower East Side. I jotted it down on my palm in pen because Max's desk was only covered in tiny empty glasses and cigar stumps.

The detective and I said our goodbyes.

Quick, easy, done.

My current victim, I mean date, was the only guy with enough guts in New York City to ask me out. I sensed a few PPD officers were feeling things out, but nobody had bothered yet, which was fine with me. I had no interest in dating someone from work. I did have my eyes on Chester, the too-young guy who manned the comic book store that hid PPD HQ from normals and hostiles. That was going nowhere fast.

"What are you smiling at?" Max asked me as I walked into the Main Room of HQ, a hellhole of noise and chaos. Officers rushed around, shouting orders, and directions, and insults.

I kept walking. I didn't have time for Max to shit on my moment of contentment. "You done with your broom handle already?" I asked.

"Don't change the subject," he yelled after me. "You find the info you were looking for?" He followed me because, of course, he couldn't let me be. I'd become his little mystery of the day.

"Yup," I said, simply. I hoped that would be the end of it.

"He taking you to dinner?"

I stopped short and turned on my heel. The flying

pixie almost crashed into my nose. I lifted a finger into his face, but he just flew up to the ceiling. "I knew there was a good reason you let me use your office, you snooping creep. You may be a good detective, Shakespeare. But you're a lousy human being!"

"I'm not a human being," he said with way too much joy.

"You know what I mean!" I yelled, as I walked toward the locker room. "Just try to be decent for once and butt out."

"Okay, okay, I get the point," he said from behind me. "Yeesh. Just pushin' yer buttons, greenie."

"Keep your hands off my buttons, Shakespeare," I said as I let the swinging door close on his face.

He pushed through and landed on top of my locker. "Just keep things on the down-low, Black," he muttered so others couldn't hear. "He's a partner to the PPD. I trust him, but we have to be careful these days."

"Meaning the enemy is everywhere."

"Exactly. I think he's a good ally. I think we need him for whatever bullshit is about to drop on this city. We need him more than yer lady parts need him."

I growled and watched the jerk fly off, donning his jerk smirk. "See you at the dance tonight," he hollered over his shoulder as he pushed his way through the door. "Save one for me."

"I'll save one for you, all right!" I yelled at the swaying door. Max's laughter flapped into the room with each swing.

CHAPTER 3

I put Holmes' height at six-two, but that guess was from memory. As I stood outside the Italian restaurant in the pouring rain, I spotted him jogging across the street, and he was definitely not six-two.

He was more like six-six.

At the moment, it didn't matter how big he was. The six-six jackass had kept me waiting. I'd planned a bunch of insults just for the hell of it, but as he walked up to me, all smiles, I forgot them all.

"Sorry I'm late," he said, shaking the water out of his hair as he moved under the canopy.

"Yeah?" I asked. I peered at him from under the edge of my crappy umbrella. "How sorry?"

"I'll treat," he said with a big smile. A smile that reached his eyes, damn it. I tried to hold onto my mild grumpiness. He had to pay for the etiquette felony.

"I was expecting that anyway," I said through a restrained grin.

"Old-fashioned, huh?" He moved closer to me with that awesome fucking smile-y, eye-y thing going on.

I backed up a step so I could keep eye contact. "If you call wanting to be dry on a first date *old-fashioned*, sure."

"Why are you waiting out here anyway?" He glanced over my head and saw the packed restaurant behind me. The waiting area was shoulder-to-shoulder with hungry New Yorkers. "Oh."

"Yeah, oh," I said, gently poking him in the shoulder. "Luckily, I've got this thing to keep me dry." I held up one of those cheap umbrellas you buy off the street from mysterious men in raincoats. The ones that magically appear after the first drop hits the pavement. The useless things magically fall apart after getting hit by the first raindrop. "Can you arrest the asshole who sold this to me?"

He smiled and held his umbrella over me. "Next time just go inside and tell them you're with me."

"Next time? What makes you think there's going to be a next time?"

"Shit," he said, looking worried. "I fucked up that bad, huh?"

"There's still time to recover," I said with a shrug, "but it sure as hell won't happen out here."

"Oh, sorry," he blurted out. He hopped past me and opened the door.

A short, fat man near the reception desk spotted my date and his face went from grumpy New Yorker to happy, short, fat man.

"Detective!" the man yelled. He was loud enough to make the restaurant chatter fade a bit. New Yorkers like to do two things: One, talk. Two, talk. Three, ignore disturbances as if they aren't happening. And four, count badly.

Holmes smiled a big grin. "Hey, Louie. Got a table open?"

Right to the point.

Nice.

"Always for you, detective!" Louie yelled. I think yelling was just natural to him. He gently slapped the back of a diner, who quickly grabbed his plate and scurried off. "Please, miss."

"That was his spot," I said, pointing my thumb at the guy who had collected himself at the small bar.

"Him?" His friendly expression went sour like a disapproving parent. "Georgie's got a tab the size of my cazzo." He gestured to his crotch with both hands.

"So you're saying he doesn't have a tab?" Holmes asked with a smirk.

Louie laughed loud enough to make the hanging wine glasses in the bar tinkle. He pulled a chair out for me.

"Thanks," I said. Holmes sat across from me and wiped his face with a cloth napkin that was immediately replaced by one of the many waiters running around. I must have looked as drenched as I felt, because my date handed me the napkin. I dried off my face and arms. I moved on to my bare legs and caught him staring. "Last time I wear a dress on a date with you."

"That's too bad," he said, leaning forward on the table.

"Yeah? You like leaving me waiting in the rain alone so I can get wet?"

I smiled, just in case he didn't know I was fooling

around. He appreciated the clue, as his face went from worried to relaxed.

He leaned back in his chair and sighed. "So, how's Max doing?"

"He's driving everyone nuts," I said, eyes rolling, "as usual."

"You guys making any progress on your side of things?"

"We here to talk about work?" I asked as I handed his napkin back.

"You're right." He pushed an imaginary button on the table. "Reset. So, where do you come from?"

It was weird he was asking me about my past. The NYPD had to stay on top of PPD business. I assumed the detective would know everything about me.

"South," I said. Maybe it was Max's warning earlier. Maybe it was my natural distrust of anyone with a heartbeat, but whatever it was, I found myself unsure how to talk about myself.

This dating stuff was tougher than I thought.

"Yeah?"

I realized how little we'd be able to talk about, being that I wasn't ready to talk about my past. Not yet. I had to change the subject. "Where are you from?" I asked.

He crossed his arms. "So are you being mysterious, or an asshole?"

The twinkle in his eye told me he wasn't angry, but I was afraid things could go sour if I wasn't careful.

"Both. Let me guess. You're from New York right?"

"Is it obvious?" he asked, tapping his knee.

"You're a straight-talker. So, yeah, pretty obvious."

"Queens," he said. I couldn't help notice how he puffed his chest out, proudly. "Born and raised. I've never been out of New York City, actually. How did you get caught up in this line of work? Or are you going to make me go look you up in the database?"

"You haven't already?"

He smiled. "I like to keep things mysterious."

I let the jab go. If I wanted to have a good time, I needed to ditch the defensive attitude. For a long moment, the date night hung on the edge of an abyss. His eyes locked on mine. I almost looked away, but caught myself and leaned forward on the table.

"I wanted to be an officer my whole life," I said. "Long as I can remember anyway. I'd check out every book on policing I could find at the library. One of my teachers had an uncle on the force, so I always helped her out around the house on holidays when he visited her. I had a huge collection of cardboard guns that I made with a friend of mine and we'd pretend to save the world from the bad guys."

"You people do have a hell of a selection of bad guys," he said.

I smiled.

The sounds of the restaurant took over. The clinking of glassware and tapping of silverware as it stabbed and scooped up the food stole our attention. Holmes was willing to let the silence linger. I was more of a chatterbox when it came to social situations. I held my tongue and kept my eyes on his, until we both smiled.

A waiter poured water in our glass goblets.

"I get it," I said, taking a sip. "I'm curious, too, Detective."

"John." He raised his glass.

"John," I said, with maybe a little too much joy. I tapped his goblet with mine. "How did you get mixed up with Max?"

He almost swallowed wrong.

"So we're back to talking about work?" he asked with a small cough.

"It looks like we have to start there."

"Let's see. Oh yeah. He was assigned to me. I had no idea what I was getting myself into. As far as I was concerned, it was just a routine interdepartmental robbery investigation."

"Then the monsters showed up?"

"Something like that. I thought the whole paranormal thing was NYPD rookie hazing. I can be dense sometimes." He glanced around to see if anyone was in earshot. Everyone was, but they were too busy yelling over each other to hear anything but themselves. "The perp had some kind of ability to make things blow up. Just out of the blue. Boom."

"Wizard, probably."

He shook his head. "I leave that stuff up to Max. I'm just there to watch his back."

"What do you mean?"

"I like Max, but he can be—"

"A fucker."

He laughed. "Yeah. You sure you're not from New York? He and I work well together, but only if I stay out of his way. Makes me more of a sidekick than a department liaison."

"You helped us in Central Park when you got us to the bunker entrance."

"I help out when I can," he said, with a shrug.

"Don't let him get to you. Buck up!" It was meant as a joke, but his face tensed up. "Sorry. I didn't mean—"

"It's fine." He smirked and pushed his chair back. "Be right back. Have to skip to the loo."

I watched him go and called myself a million nasty names, including a slick-lipped, no-class, bigfoot-in-mouth mother fucker. Buck up? Really?

"Smooth move, rookie," a voice said from nearby. It was hard to tell where it came from with all the noise in the room. I knew Max's voice when I heard it, but he was nowhere in sight. I chalked it up to imagination.

Then my backpack moved.

"You are fucking kidding me," I mumbled. I opened it and Max, sandwiched between my wallet and sunglasses case, grinned up at me. "What are you doing here, asshole?"

"Making sure you don't screw up and make an interdepartmental mess. What any good partner would do."

"You have a really fucked up definition of what a good partner is, pixie."

"Good job, so far." He was giving me two thumbs up and a big grin. "I would work on the humor though. It's gonna be a short night if you keep letting your feline sass hang out."

I felt eyes on me and looked up to see the guy at the

bar staring at me like I was nuts. I *was* talking to my open purse after all. I pulled a small mirror out and worked on my lipstick. That gave me some leeway to move my mouth around a little bit as I tore my partner a new one.

"How about I show up at your pub and comment on… whatever it is you do over there?"

"You're welcome anytime," he said. "Just be sure to bring a raincoat."

"Okay, first of all, I don't want to know what the hell that means." I pretended to wipe my mouth with the napkin to hide my moving lips. "Second, you need to get out of here. I passed your test, so it's time for you to leave."

"Okay, okay, spoil sport," he said as he closed the backpack's zipper.

I snapped up my bag, threw it over my shoulder, and slipped out of the restaurant. The rain was coming down hard, but that didn't stop me from yanking the pack open again and dumping my partner on the sidewalk. I'm not sure what half the words were that came out of his mouth, but I enjoyed the sight of Shakespeare flying off into the night sky, doing his best to weave between the raindrops.

CHAPTER 4

*J*ohn was back at our table as I slipped into the booth across from him.

"You okay?" he asked, shoving my chair out with his foot.

"Yeah," I said, unable to make eye contact. "Just went out for a breath of fresh air."

"Louie said you were talking to your purse."

"Is that a problem?"

He looked at me like he was figuring me out. I didn't smile, but he did. That was probably the moment I was hooked on Holmes.

"You're a funny woman," he said.

"Do you like funny women?"

He shrugged. "I like you."

I raised my glass. "Good answer."

The rest of the meal went way too well. Like jinxed well. The kind of well that only happens when the fecal matter's about to slam into oscillating blades of steel. I enjoyed every second of it, and tried to shut up the little

JOHN P. LOGSDON & BEN ZACKHEIM

voice in my head that said, "Enjoy it while you can, sweetheart!"

John paid the check, helped me get my coat on and popped the umbrella open as we stepped out into the downpour. A cab drove by and he whistled. The car skidded to a stop and Holmes opened the door for me. I could get used to that treatment. It was so kind, and smooth.

And unusual.

The feeling of being tended to was usually something I associated with The Zoo, my previous home where I'd been kept safe by guards and bureaucracy. But this was a different feeling.

With Holmes, I felt safe and welcome.

And even more amazing, I felt welcoming.

The cab pulled to the curb. I'd been so deep in thought that we hadn't spoken a word for the entire ride. I didn't wait for him to open my door. I slipped across the faux leather seat and stepped onto the sidewalk. The rain had stopped, leaving a welcome sweetness to the air.

"That's the dance hall?" I asked Holmes.

He shrugged and looked up at the steeple of the former church on 16th street. "It's used for private events now. We've broken up a few raves here, actually."

The two of us walked up the wide stone stairs and pushed through the tall doors.

The high ceilings made the place feel bigger than the city outside. It took my breath away and gave me a feeling of openness I hadn't felt since I'd been a New Yorker. I didn't know if God was in that place, but someone cool had left their mark on it.

"Wow," was all I could say. One glance at John, and I could tell he was also impressed.

"Yeah, I like it here," he said. "It's nifty."

That made me stop walking. "Nifty?"

He stopped and turned to me. "Yeah. Nifty. What's wrong with nifty?"

"Nothing, if you're 92 years old."

He shrugged. "I like to bring back old words. It's a hobby of mine."

"That's a bunch of poppycock," I said.

He smiled down at me, eyebrows raised. Game on. "I didn't know you were such a wisenheimer," he said.

"Oh, you did too. Don't give me that applesauce."

"What are you two giggling at?" Max asked from behind us.

I tried to wipe the smile from my face. I was still pissed at my partner for intruding earlier. "Just some jiggery-pokery," I said with a snort-laugh to top it off.

Holmes laughed, too. I guess I couldn't take my eyes off of him because the smile faded and he asked, "What?"

"Nothing."

"Oy vey!" Max yelled as he floated over our heads to join the growing crowd. "I'll leave you two alone."

"About time!" I shouted.

"How do you put up with him?" John asked.

We started walking down the stairs to the main party area. "I'm not easy to get along with, either," I said with a shrug. "I try to keep that in mind when I want to stomp on him like a bug."

"I don't know," John said. "I think you're pretty pleasant."

My eyes probably widened a bit. "No one's ever accused me of being pleasant."

"It's not an accusation."

"It is in my book." He clearly didn't know what to say. I could see him racking his brain for a response. "See?" I said. "Unpleasant!"

He laughed. "You already told me you love to dance. But are you any good at it?"

I had a dilemma. Should I tell him I'd never been to a dance before? All my dancing had been in front of a mirror. I wanted to set expectations. Low, low, low expectations. "You probably won't make it out of tonight alive."

"I'll settle for deformed," John said.

I nodded my head. "I'll try to tone down my twirls then. Maybe we could limit the damage to a few missing fingers."

"How's it hangin', kid?" Bob yelled from halfway across the church. My goblin bodyguard slinked through the crowd toward us.

"Watch what you say around Bob," I muttered. "It will be used against you later."

"Duly noted," John mumbled back.

Bob rushed up to us and studied my date like he was a bomb that needed to be defused. "This the guy, BB?" the goblin asked.

My date nodded his head and smiled. Classy guy. I cleared my throat and tried not to cuss my goblin bodyguard out.

"Bob, this is Detective Holmes," I said.

"You can call me John," Holmes said.

The noise of the room was drowned out by Bob's laughing.

"John Holmes," Bob choked out between laughs. "Your parents should be sued."

"Not as funny as your face," Holmes said, annoyed. I chuckled.

"Awright, awright," Bob yelled. "Sorry, buddy. Yeesh. Lou! Get over here! BB's man-thing is here! Break away from the food table, ya jerkoff!"

"BB! Wassup, girl? This John?"

"How did you know his name?" I asked.

"I did some digging, sweetheart. Gotta make sure you're attracted to the right kinda fellas, right?"

"Yeah, but do you know his last name, Lou?" Bob asked.

"Holmes."

"John Holmes!" Bob said, smirking. But Lou didn't show any sign of getting the joke. "Get it? The porn star? Hung like a troll."

"Nah, you know I don't get your jokes, Bob." Lou turned to us. "You two need to try the shrimp. They explode in your mouth."

"Sounds...good," Holmes said.

"I know another shrimp I'd like to explode," Bob snarled.

"Be nice!" Lou hollered. "We need to make a good impression for BB!"

"Too late," I mumbled.

My date glanced down at me and smiled. He took my hand and pulled softly. I smiled back and we sidestepped away from the argument.

"I am being nice!" Bob yelled back, sticking his long finger in his cousin's face. "You should see what an asshole I'm being in my head!"

Lou stuck his own skinny finger in Bob's face. "Yer head is an asshole! One steady stream o' shit just pourin' out!"

I stood on my tiptoes and whispered to John, "Good move."

"Hey, save me a dance, BB," a man's voice said from behind us. It was Chester, the stunner from the comic book store. I didn't know where he'd come from. He glanced up at John and smirked. John didn't look pleased. "Hey, hey," Chester said, holding up his hands in a peaceful gesture. "Chill. Just one dance, buddy. Bethany and I are just friends." John tried to act civil, but he didn't do a good job of it. His mouth smiled and his eyes stabbed.

"Chester, this is John," I said, stepping back so they could shake hands. "I'll definitely save you a dance. Let me break this guy in first." I winked, and Chester bowed his head and moved on.

The music waned as a new song was about to start.

"Perfect segue into my bad moves," John said. "Want to dance?"

"Yeah!" Too excited and nervous. "Yes," I said softer.

He led me to the dance floor where a few of the bolder officers were trying to make it a real party.

I hoped for a fast song. I didn't want to do the whole close thing yet. Well, I did, but it was too soon. Luckily, a heavy beat started up and an electric guitar dropped in like a hammer.

I was delighted and horrified to see that he was as bad a dancer as I was.

He jumped up and down, straight as a board, with his arms straight to his side. I think he learned his moves from the old Charlie Brown cartoons.

At least he wasn't puckering his lips and swaying his hips like a dingy floating in choppy water like me.

"What the fuck is that she doin'?" I heard Bob mutter to Lou. They'd stopped their argument to discuss our dancing styles.

"They look like a couple of escaped pile drivers," Lou said. I couldn't tell if they intended for us to hear.

We didn't care.

It was fun.

We knew we were bad. Together we were worse. Let everyone have their laughs. It was at their expense.

The music suddenly stopped and a slow, mellow song took over. I glanced at the DJ. He was reaching for the music controls, but Max shoved him back with a nudge to the forehead.

Max had taken over the music selection.

My partner wore an "I'm a fucker" smirk on his face, as the people who had been watching us dance like we were the only people in the world, now expected us to go slow.

Holmes held out his hand. He must have seen my fear and anger and thirst for bloody revenge on my face because he grinned slightly and jerked his head in a 'come on' kind of way.

So I went on.

He pulled me close and wrapped his left hand around

my waist. It went half way around me. It was then it hit me how big he was. I thought of looking up at him. I knew that once I did, I'd be in it deep.

But Sarge and his posse of old-men PPD brass caught my eye. Their serious faces brought me down to earth. Hard.

Suddenly, I wondered what the hell we were all doing there. What about the part-goblin, part-tiger army of Goblers that were out in the city somewhere, growing, getting stronger? Their existence threatened everything I loved. The PPD, New York, Mike, my friends.

So why the hell were we all dancing as if everything was normal?

I slapped the thought down. It wasn't a time to feel guilty. I'd been through enough pain and isolation to deserve one fucking night of fun.

I breathed into the evening as my plugged-up brain cleared out.

I felt good.

I looked up and smiled. Holmes smiled back.

We had about one second to enjoy the moment before the attack started.

CHAPTER 5

*T*hey came through the stained-glass windows.

The dozens of beautiful glass artworks shattered at exactly the same time. I didn't know what the hell was going on. I'd just been spun in circles by a six-foot-whatever cop, so that was one strike against me.

The shock of the attack was the other.

It was so sudden, I must have pulled a partial transform. My tiger senses were on high. Every bouncing, cracking, scraping piece of glass in the room overwhelmed my ears.

Until the screams drowned out everything else.

Goblers.

A dozen of the half-tiger, half-mobgoblin fuckers, at least.

They'd caught the entire department off guard, mostly unarmed, and drunk. It was a perfectly-timed attack.

I realized this could be the end of the New York PPD if we didn't fight back, and hard.

One of them jumped on me and brought five sharp

nails down at my face. I cocked my head to the left just in time to dodge the brunt of the blow. I couldn't avoid all of it, though. A razor-sharp tip slashed my cheek, blasting my whole face with a searing pain.

I went full tiger.

But the gobler must have known I was the lone weretiger officer because he was ready for me. He jumped back, just out of reach of my fangs, which chomped down on air where his head used to be. Two of his buddies dropped from the balcony above us and joined in the fun. They circled around me, walking sideways, hissing and grinning. It was a coordinated, practiced attack.

"BB," Max called out over the connector, *"I'm on my way. Hold them off!"*

"Great idea, Max. I was thinking maybe now would be a good time to clean my paws."

A small flying object slapped one of the goblers in the head. He turned to see what had hit him, but Max was already buzzing him on the other side.

"Thanks, Max. I'll take the big one."

But my date was way ahead of me. I would have been touched if Holmes hadn't tried to take the gobler out with his bare hands. Stupid move. If he was trying to impress me, he'd done the opposite. One swift move by the beast and it shoved the detective down and stood on his chest, pinning him.

Now it was up to me to save him.

My fangs found the gobler's foot and pressed in deep. The thing screeched like a banshee as my teeth broke its bones with a loud crack. It turned on me and its good foot landed in between my ribs. I heard my own bones crack and hoped the adrenaline would keep me strong until the fight was over.

The gobler swiped at my chest, barely missing. It was my first break of the night. The momentum of its swing carried through and messed up its balance. It fell toward me.

I snagged its forehead in my fangs. I shook back and forth until the gobler's head broke right off its body.

"Fuckin' A, kid," Max said. *"Didn't have enough dinner at the restaurant?"*

"Can't get it out," I screamed back. *"Can't get it out of my mouth!"*

The head was too big for my jaws and a few of my fangs were stuck to… something. I was full tiger, so I was caught between enjoying my meal, and not wanting to think about the details of what I was swallowing.

Max flew down and grabbed the decapitated gobler's hair and yanked. It didn't budge. I spotted a nearby gobler watching all of this happen. His eyes were wide. That was an important moment because it taught me something about our attackers.

The goblers had a sense of self-preservation. They weren't the savage beasts we'd battled in Central Park.

Bob and Lou joined the tug-of-war until the head popped from my jaws. It arced through the air and landed at the feet of some advancing goblers. They stopped short and hesitated for a moment.

Just long enough for Bob and Lou and Holmes to open fire. The goblers scattered, and we had the first advantage of the night.

It would also be our last.

The beasts ran into the dark corners of the ex-church and disappeared into the shadows like ghosts. Again, the move was coordinated. Even their defense was well-planned. A sense of awe and fear flowed over me and, from the looks on their faces, the rest of the PPD too. There were a couple dozen of us left. We were fighting drunk, injured, unprepared.

But we were pros, and we were ready.

Without a word, we all moved quickly into a circle, facing outward. We watched for any movement from the edges of the large room.

"Anything moves, shoot it," Max said with a growl in his voice.

A figure stumbled into view and fell to the floor, face down. A dozen of us aimed but didn't fire. It was Sarge. A couple of officers went to retrieve him. They each grabbed a hand and tugged the boss toward us.

Everything happened so fast, it was impossible to see. It was impossible to stop. The two officers dragging Sarge suddenly screamed in agony and fell to the floor. They slid into the darkness like they were being dragged by something unseen.

Sarge still lay on the floor, not moving.

"What the hell was that?" Max asked everyone, but no one answered. No one knew.

We couldn't empty any rounds into the shadows. Not unless we wanted to put our comrades at risk.

There was only one thing we could do. One thing I could do.

I jumped into the nearest shadow and crouched low.

Something was bugging me about the attack, besides

the whole fighting-for-our-lives thing. But I couldn't figure out what.

"You'd better know what yer doing, kid," Max said.

"You know me better than that, Max," I replied.

I rounded the corner near the front of the room, where the dais would be if it had still been a holy place. As opposed to the gate to hell it had become.

The whimpering of injured officers was all I could hear. I could see movement in the opposite corner.

"The goblers are bunched together in the southeast corner of the room," I said. *"About a dozen of them. They're standing as still as statues in some kind of defensive formation."*

"Where are the officers?"

"I don't know. I can't see them. I can smell their fear, though."

"I think that's my shorts," Max said. *"Move in close and get a twenty on them. If you can't, then make a guess based on the goblers' behavior."*

"Got it."

I slinked ahead as silently as the pads on my paws would let me. I kept my breathing low, quiet. I was in stalking mode, which is a tough one to beat when you're the prey.

They beat me anyway.

Four of their silhouetted heads snapped to the right to face me.

Busted.

I had one chance to make some chaos of my own. I jumped at them and ran directly into a gobler who leapt at me. Now I understood the defensive position. Now I saw their plan. They'd bunched up in a corner with two of our own to focus our attention where they'd wanted it. Their top fighter was now on top of me, trying to stick her fangs into my neck, while the rest of them scattered down the dark aisles of the church. Their plan depended on one of the officers losing his cool and firing. That would start a volley of shots into the dark corner where I'd told my friends they were hiding.

Were, being the key word.

The goblers had scattered.

"Don't shoot!" I yelled over our connection.

An officer shot. A volley followed.

I spotted our officers' bodies jerking around from the dozens of rounds of friendly fire that tore them apart. The goblers had moved on to other attack positions.

I lucked out and got a mouthful of my attacker's shoulder in my mouth. I turned that into a chance to stick my magic claws in her back. The sound of her flesh pulling apart set off a hunger in me. A hunger for more than revenge. A hunger for meat.

The officers were dead. There was no doubt about it. But I'd make sure every single one of those goblin fuckers paid with painful deaths.

I shoved the dying gobler off of me and shook her blood from my face and back. The room had become a slaughterhouse. The PPD was fighting hard, but we were losing bad. The ones who teamed up in small groups were able to hold on longer, but they were being picked off one-by-one.

Right when I saw no hope for us, another gobler busted through a window and landed on the balcony above.

She was huge.

From the dress, I assumed she was a she. The giant looked down on the chaos from the balcony like a parent making sure the kids were behaving. Or, in this case, misbehaving to the point of murder. She moved around as if she were on wheels — one smooth line, straight ahead, without a trace of bounce to her step.

One thing was clear. She was the leader.

"Max," I said, *"up in the balcony. She looks like the leader."*

"I see her."

"On three," I stated. Max jumped the gun. He flew at her like a shot. *"Okay, then. On one, I guess."*

I joined in with a leap of my own that took me to the stairs leading up to her perch. My claws were having a tough time grabbing onto the stone floor. I reached the top of the staircase and slid into the wall. I bounced off in the right direction and found my balance fast.

I sprinted at the gobler, who was fending Max off with moves that were as smooth as her walk.

It was some kind of martial art, but I couldn't be sure which one. Whatever it was, it was effective. Max's decision to distract her with his favorite 'Act Like a Bug and Bug The Bad Guy' move wasn't a good one. He should have used his guns to give me my opening. She slapped him three times and landed a good kick before I could reach them.

Not that my contribution did anything to help.

My front claws were stretched out as my back legs pushed off the floor with enough strength to barrel through a rhino. My magic claws glowed blue, ready to pierce through flesh or steel.

She had her back to me. Max was on the floor in front of her, scrambling back on his butt.

It's amazing how many thoughts we can pack into a millisecond. As I reached for the gobler, the thought that broke through all of the others was...

I'm too late.

CHAPTER 6

*M*ama Gobler turned on one heel and brought the other foot up in my face. It was a perfectly timed kick.

It felt like my head snapped off of my body as the momentum of my jump stopped hard. I dropped to the floor and scampered around. My claws needed to find somewhere to stick or I was going to be a fish in a barrel.

I looked up just in time to see her landing on me. One foot buried itself into my stomach. Then the other foot landed on my tail.

Her ugly mug managed to convey a smile. It was hard to read with that fang-filled snout.

But it wasn't the face that scared me.

It was the look she gave me.

It was smart. It was calculating. It was measuring me, gauging my response.

I curled my feline body and snapped at her foot. She dodged it easily. I tried to slip my right front leg between her legs to trip her and bring her down toward my eager fangs. She lifted her leg and brought it down on my tail again.

She was toying with me.

So, I toyed with her.

I went Full Human.

I felt the pain of her attacks more acutely, which sucked, but I also had two free hands and a 6er. I grabbed the weapon from my hip holster and got off a shot before she could screw up my aim.

Bullseye.

Right in the head.

Too bad that didn't kill her.

She screeched and shook her head as she backed toward a wall. She slammed into it and tore at her face. I thought she was going nuts, but then she turned to face me, smirked, and threw something in my direction.

It clinked on the stone floor and rolled toward my feet.

She'd pulled the bullet from her own skull.

I fired again, but missed.

She took advantage and ducked into the deep shadows around us. I could hear her scampering under the arches that lined both sides of the church. She was putting as much space between me and her as she could.

I couldn't let her get away.

"You okay, BB?" Max asked.

"Beat up, but okay. I shot the boss lady in the face."

"Good job!"

"She's still on her feet."

"Shit."

"I think she's headed toward the front of the church. Try to

head her off." Max didn't respond in his usual snappy voice. *"Max? You get that?"*

Again, no answer. Something smacked into the wall behind me and hit the floor with a thud.

It was Max.

He was semi-conscious. Blood poured from his little cheek. I tried to apply pressure to the wound, but he thrashed around. I had no idea how to treat an injured pixie. He moved his head back and forth as if he were trying to wake himself up.

"Max?" He opened his eyes and looked at me like he didn't know me.

He squinted and wiped his eyes with one hand. "Ugh. Not what I want to see first thing in the morning."

"One, it's not first thing in the morning, asshole. Two, you're an asshole. You okay?"

He felt his cheek, which was swelling up in front of my eyes. "I'm fine, rookie. You?"

"She beat me up pretty good, but I think I'm okay."

Max hopped up and took to the air, hovering over me with that permanently-pissed frown on his face. "Where's the boss gobler?"

We moved to the balcony to get a view of the chaos below. I had to steal a moment to catch my breath. The goblers were engaged in hand-to-hand combat with my fellow officers.

It was not going well.

Sarge and his posse of PPD brass were all out cold, or worse. Their bodies were strewn all over the church floor, where minutes before we'd all managed to have a good time. Silly us. The PPD was one tough place to work.

"Something is wrong," Max said.

"Yeah, I was thinking the same thing." I got the lay of the land, and I didn't like what I saw. "They want us."

"No shit. Any other gems stuck in that head of yers waiting to come out?"

"No, Max," I said, pointing to him and then to myself. "They want us. Our team."

"What the hell does that mean?"

"Look." He followed my pointing finger down to Graham and Fay. The two of them stood alone in the middle of the room, unarmed and back-to-back. No one had attacked them. One gobler was keeping them in one small area. 'Herding' might be a better word.

Max growled, "They're pushing everyone else to the wall."

It was true. The goblers weren't fighting our forces anymore, as much as they were *guiding* them.

"They're going to trap them and slaughter them," I said.

"Not if I can do anything about it. Get to the middle of the room! NOW!" The urgency in his voice told me all I needed to know. He'd come to the same conclusion I had. We had to get the goblers' attention. We had to take their focus off the others and make them fight us.

The idea of more PPD officers dying en masse filled me with a heated dread that burned through my gut. We were still recovering from the attack on New York that had taken out half our force. It was before I was taken on, but the battle's impact on the NY PPD would last for years.

I especially didn't like the idea of more officers dying

because the goblers wanted to get their paws on me and my team.

I ran down the stairs and joined Max, Graham and Fay. I handed Fay my second firearm and Max handed Graham his dinky version of a Glock handgun. We joked behind Max's back that it was more like a Glick. Graham tried to get a handle on the small grip and accidentally fired off a round.

"Careful, rookie," Max yelled over his shoulder. "Now you've got two bullets left."

"He can't hear you, Max," I muttered.

"I don't need to hear him to know he's tearing me a new one," Graham said, looking at me. He winked.

"I'm going to open those doors from the outside," Max said under his breath. "It'll give the others a chance to escape." Max floated above our heads. "You rookies try not to die."

"That's helpful, oh wise teacher," I mumbled. He didn't hear me. Max was already out the window and off to execute his plan. It was a good one, but it required us to pull the goblers toward us. The three of us faced outward, weapons drawn and waited for a clear shot at the enemy. But our fellow officers were in the line of fire. Our weapons had been neutralized.

Or had they?

I spotted a chandelier hanging over the middle of the room. I aimed and fired at the ceiling above it. The shot didn't get any attention. The place was too noisy for a single shot to steal their attention. But the second shot hit its mark, sending the plaster ceiling down in large chunks.

The chandelier swayed back and forth, jerked and fell to the stone floor with a deafening shatter.

The goblers' sensitive ears worked in our favor. A few of them cringed, grasping their ears, and fell down, curled up in pain. A few others had the fortitude to stumble into the shadows, out of view.

Suddenly, the door behind the PPD officers opened with a loud creak. The officers realized it was their only chance to escape the night alive and joined together to pull it open wide. They slipped through just as the remaining goblers got to their feet.

Graham, Fay and I yelled at the goblers to stay down on the ground. It was our duty to take unarmed assailants into custody. If we could grab one of them it would be a small victory.

Four of the beasts gathered their senses in front of us. That's when I noticed, for the first time, that they were decked out in spiffy suits and dresses. What was it with goblers and fashion? Three of them ran off so fast we couldn't even get a shot off. The fourth one, working an Armani suit, was seconds from having enough sense to run away.

So I shot him in the gut.

He heaved out gallons of oxygen and fell back onto the stone floor in a fetal position.

"He'll live. Fay, Graham, cover him while I…"

I didn't get a chance to finish my sentence. The sound of shattered glass from above our heads made sure of that. I caught a glimpse of Mama Goblin's large shape jumping through an ex-window. Then I heard something that chilled my heart in an instant.

A distant scream.

"Max!" I yelled through the connection. *"I think the leader snagged one of our officers. I'm going after her."* I holstered my 6er and went full tiger again. I hoped it would be the last time I had to do that for a while. The transformation was starting to wear me down, but if I were honest with myself, I was also afraid of the growing urge to be a cat. Something in me was pushing to be feline full-time. With every change, I felt closer to my tiger side.

The more I let the tiger in, the less I'd be Officer Black.

CHAPTER 7

*B*y the time I got to the windowsill, the gobler boss was gone.

I sniffed out her scent, a cross between new clothing, Dior perfume and light sweat. Not exercise sweat. Nervous sweat.

Good.

She should have been nervous. I planned to take her out hard. In fact, I planned to use her as a message to the other goblers.

You may have some weretiger in you, but my claws dig deeper.

The roof of the church's abbey, now a residential building, was about two floors below us. I saw a large dent in the tar roof where the gobler had landed. I couldn't see her anywhere, but she was close. And she was slower than me. The hostage would make her easy to catch. I trotted to the edge of the balcony to get the most running room and then sprinted. My paws crunched on

41

the broken glass until I planted my back claws in the carpeted floor and pushed off.

I covered the distance easily. Actually, I overshot the roof by a couple of feet. I reached out my front claws and managed to snag a window frame on the top floor. I hung on it for dear life. I would have apologized to the nice old lady in her bed watching porn, if I'd been in human form. My legs flailed around until they found a claw-hold. I climbed up the brick exterior and peeked over the edge of the roof.

Stupid move.

I had to settle down.

I also had to be quick and, somehow, give the bitch no cause to harm her hostage, whoever it was.

I lifted my nose to the air and opened my mouth to taste the scents around me. I caught the sour smell of perfume on goblin skin. I didn't know what the hell was up with the goblers' love of fashion, but it was undeniable they all shared a taste for expensive duds. I couldn't be sure it was the leader's odor, but it came from nearby.

It was my best lead.

I scrambled up the steep roof of the abbey to get a better perspective. I hopped across three gargoyles to reach an even steeper area. The slope was tough, but claw followed claw until I reached the top.

Under any other circumstance I would have loved that view. The river and Brooklyn spread out over the horizon on one side of me, and the entirety of Manhattan rolled into the distance like a parade of lights and life. The sound of a pained grunt broke the spell and made me look behind me and down. Two rooftops away, I spotted my target and her payload. She did have one of us. He or she was thrown over Mama Gobler's broad shoulders.

"*You okay, BB?*" Fay asked me over the connection.

It was good to hear her voice, especially since she'd been angry with me since the Club One incident where I'd gone along with Max's performance as a turncoat PPD officer.

"*Fine. I see Mama Gobler. She's taking a bitch-break on a building nearby.*"

"*Be right there,*" Max said.

"*No, I need to take this one alone. If she senses us coming, she may kill the officer.*"

"*Any idea who it is?*" Graham asked.

"*Not yet. But they're definitely in deep shit if I can't get to them, so no more questions, okay?*"

The radio silence helped me focus as I scrambled down the slate tiles. My claws scraped a bit. Not a welcome noise, but it couldn't be helped. I dropped to the abbey's lower roof and jumped across an alley to the roof of the building near my target. I crept to the edge and could just make out the gobler below me, hunched over her prize. I couldn't tell what she was doing, but I knew it couldn't be anything good. I couldn't shake the feeling that I was too late. But I wouldn't let that discourage me. I scanned the roof below for a good landing spot and saw a water tower directly across.

Perfect.

I landed on the roof and splayed my paws on the wood surface. It was an awkward touchdown. One claw bent the wrong way, sending a shot of pain through my leg that almost made me snarl. But I kept my mouth shut and my landing was quiet enough to blend in with the New York City din. That's all that counted.

"Hello, bitch," a gravelly woman's voice said from below me. "Welcome to the party."

The gobler was waiting for me.

I walked to the edge of the water tower and growled at what I saw. Mama Gobler stood behind my friend Chester with one long claw jammed into his neck.

His face showed me all I needed to know.

One of the things Max taught me early was that a victim of kidnapping always knows better than you what their captor is capable of. Something in the victim gives them the information they need to know when they're about to bite the dust.

Chester's face had some bad news.

He was convinced that she was going to kill him.

She smirked and held up a Glock with her free hand, perfectly aimed between my eyes.

She wanted to kill me first, I guess.

I jumped to the side and the bullet grazed a hind leg. It hurt, but it was no big deal. I had more to worry about with the second shot. I landed on the gravel roof and pushed off to the right. The second bullet skipped off the stones and smacked into the wooden wall of a pigeon cage. The birds flurried around at the sound.

I faced the beast, and she turned the gun on Chester's temple.

"Now I have options," she said. Her voice had a low rumble to it, like a growl was added to every word. "I can take him out fast and painless, or slow and bloody. Have you ever seen someone die who knew the end was coming?" I couldn't answer her in my tiger form, but I suspected she wasn't interested in making this a dialogue. "It's a delicious thing." Yup, she answered her own question.

The scene told me two things.

One, she was nervous and she wanted to talk. She had to threaten Chester in a couple of ways because she'd never been in a standoff before. With the gun off of me, she knew I could easily escape.

Two, she was a sadistic motherfucker who would feel my claws in her ass before the night was over.

Now that I'd lost the element of surprise, I had a couple of options. I was in tiger form, so I couldn't talk her down, but I didn't think she could be talked down. She felt trapped and she was going to use Chester to get out of there, so option one was to run off and let her and her victim escape. I could track her, turn back to human form and get a bead on her with my 6er from a distance. Longshot, though. We'd probably end up in the same bind.

Option two, let the standoff play out on my terms. I decided on number two as an idea popped into my head.

I bowed my head and laid down and just stared at her. I was ready to run if she aimed the Glock at me, but I was all chill on the outside. I licked my paw and wiped my face.

I showed all the signs of a cat that was not interested in playing.

If she had enough cat infused into her goblin head, she'd know that this was all part of the feline game. But she'd also be compelled to play that game, deadly as it was. If you've ever watched two cats size each other up, you know what I'm talking about. We pretend we're not interested, float our attention around the room like everything else in the world is more interesting than you. If the alpha cat isn't ready to attack, she'll play along and feign disinterest. This could go on for hours.

I had a feeling this game would last a minute, tops.

She put the gun back into a hip holster strapped around her expensive blouse. Bingo. She was all-in.

But the claw stabbed deeper and Chester hissed in pain.

"How did you like our little surprise at the ball, Black?" Mama Goblin croaked. She knew who I was, which was another clue that the attack was coordinated to eliminate me and my team. "I'd call that a blowout, wouldn't you?"

Sure, I wanted to tear her in two, but instead I pulled some loose fur off my paw and tried to get it out of my mouth with my long tongue. I threatened to hack up a furball.

"So what now?" she asked, getting more nervous. A shot of nerves heated up my chest. All of a sudden, I had a feeling I'd chosen the wrong option. "You think I'm going to wait around for your remaining friends to arrive and help you out? Fuck you!"

I looked at her and panted. It was my way of saying, "Whatever, bitch." I keyed in on her left elbow because her left hand's claw was an inch deep in Chester's neck. If that elbow showed signs of tensing up, I'd know she was going for the kill. Chester was getting nervous. He couldn't tell what was going on. I was getting nervous, too.

A pigeon let out a faint chirp. That gave me an idea. I

slapped the cage with my tail. The birds started freaking out again. I pointed my nose at the cage and sniffed. I shifted my body just a little bit so I was facing the cage.

"Don't fucking move," the gobler yelled, but I was already facing the cage and playfully swiping at the frantic birds. They flew to the back corner of the cage to get away from me. I nudged the door handle with my nose and the wood peg slid out of its slot. The door opened and the birds fluttered around like crazy. I stepped into the cage. The gobler and Chester couldn't see in. My "plan" was to make them think I was torturing the birds. I focused my ears on any sign of footsteps on gravel. If I heard that, then there was a good chance she was trying to escape.

"Looks like your friend is more interested in the birds than saving you, buddy," Mama Gobler growled.

Perfect. She bought it. I was delighted with myself and listened for the sound of her fleeing footsteps.

"So I guess this is goodbye," she said.

I heard Chester let out a quick dry gasp. It got wet fast as I heard the claw dig through my friend's artery and into his throat.

CHAPTER 8

I roared and leaned hard on the wood wall. It splintered under my weight.

Chester was on the ground. He jerked around as his body tried to fight the inevitable. Blood poured from his neck and mouth and overwhelmed my senses. The sight of the growing puddle behind his head, the sound of the beating flow, the smell of approaching death. I ran to him and went full human. I tried to press my palm against his wound but he was moving too violently.

"Chester! Stop! Please!"

He started to slow down but not because he heard me. It was because he was losing his strength. He was dying. I finally worked my palm onto his slick neck and pressed down as hard as I could.

"We need a medic up here! The rooftop near the old church abbey!"

"On it," Sue, the AI, responded.

I heard the gobler, now a few rooftops away, cackle loud enough for human ears. She wanted me to know she

49

had enjoyed herself. I had to work hard to stay in place. I was Chester's only chance to live. I'd make her pay another day.

"Bethany," Chester whispered, "hey."

"Hey, Chester. Hang in there, okay? Medics are on the way."

"Sorry," he said. His voice was fading.

"No, I'm sorry, I tried—"

"Sorry I didn't get a dance." He smiled and, for a moment, I thought he was going to be okay.

But the smile faded and his eyes stuck on me, unseeing.

"No!" I pressed harder in the wound. *Sue! Where's the medic?*

"Two minutes, Black!"

"We don't have two fucking minutes!"

His body went limp under my hands.

The blood stopped flowing.

I don't know how long I sat there, but I was completely lost. So when Max touched my shoulder, I jerked around and stuck my 6er in his gut.

"Hey kid," he said.

I didn't have any words in me. I turned back to Chester and realized I was still holding his hand. I'm not sure what good that did anyone, but I didn't let go, even after Max whispered, "Let them get him out of here."

I heard some shuffling from behind me and turned to see Dick and Pat, the medics, running across the roof toward me. Dick was massive. Every step he took shook the whole building. They reached us, took one look at Chester, and their shoulders slumped.

I stepped away so they could try to do the impossible. I walked to the edge of the roof where the gobler had escaped.

Laughing.

Her laughter was a hot rod through my heart. I couldn't take the rage.

"Whoa," Max yelled from beside me. "Black! Settle down!"

"What's the problem, Max?"

"Your whole head was full tiger for a second, rookie. Is that normal? There's no way that's normal, right?"

"Just my head?"

That seemed to make him uncomfortable for some reason. "It's not like I could see if you had seventy-two nipples or whatever."

"What the fuck, Shakespeare? I mean my legs. My arms. Is your head always way down in the pits of filth?"

"Just yer head."

"That's not normal, no," I said. "Last time anything like that happened was in our fight with Baudelaire. But that was a spell." I left it at that. It wasn't time to go over all the shitty things it could mean. I didn't like the idea of losing my ability to control my transformations, but it wasn't the time to worry. I looked off to the horizon. "She went that way."

"Think we could catch her?"

I shook my head. "She was faster than me. Even with Chester in her arms, she was tough to catch."

"We'll get her, Black."

We locked eyes. I nodded.

Dick lifted Chester's body from the bloody tar. They'd

wrapped him in a body bag. The giant medic looked over at me. He was crying.

"KITTY'S FRIEND?" he asked with a voice that always matched his size.

I smiled at him and started crying too.

Max landed on the ground next to me. "It's not your fault, kid."

"I made a bad call. It is my fault."

"Bad calls don't make it your fault unless you're the one kidnapping or killing. This is the gobler's doing. Not yours. Want to tell me what happened now?"

I shoved a sob down and shook my head. I made a beeline for the fire escape.

"It's over," Max told me as I descended the rickety steps.

"Did we lose anyone else?" I asked.

"I don't know. But…"

"But what?"

"It's too fucking familiar, is all," he said under his breath.

I knew what he meant. We'd just lost half the NY PPD force a few months before. The wounds from the massacre were wide open that night.

I dropped from the last rung of the ladder and landed in the filth of a New York alley. The city had cleaned itself up a lot recently, but the alleys were still a breeding ground for new forms of shit.

"You look like I feel," I said to the ground beneath my feet.

"Bethany," Fay yelled from the end of the alley. "You're

okay!" She ran at me and wrapped her tiny arms around me. Or halfway around me.

"Graham?" I asked her.

"He's okay. He's pissed."

"Yeah, I'm with him on that. What's the status back at the church?"

Her relief at seeing me alive faded from her face. "Still counting our losses." She left it at that.

We walked from the alley and met with a wall of NYPD, headed up by my date. He spotted me too and broke away from his fellow officers. He didn't run at me, but his strides were the size of me. He slowed down when he realized I was walking with my team. His steps got awkward as if he was thinking about turning the other way and running.

"Hey," I said.

"Hi. Hey. You're okay."

"I lost a friend."

"Oh. I'm sorry."

"We should leave these two alone," Max said.

If it had come out of anyone else's mouth, it would have been sweet, but, as usual, he pumped in an extra few gallons of sass.

"No," John said, maybe a little too sharply. "I should get back. You..." he muttered, looking down at me. "I'll call you."

"Yeah?" I asked. "Looking forward to our next date?"

"Not really," he said and smiled. That gave me a jolt of something. I'm not sure what. Joy? Me and joy weren't too familiar with each other, so it was tough to say. I immediately felt bad about it, though. Chester was dead.

Chester was dead because I didn't do my job.

How was I going to live with that?

I watched John walk ahead of us and rejoin his team, when an angry voice slashed into my moment of peace.

"It would have helped if we weren't a bunch of fucking idiots!"

It was Graham.

"Excuse me?" I asked, turning to him to make sure he could see my pissed-off face. "What the hell is that supposed to mean?"

"We're up against the biggest threat in PPD history, and we threw a fucking ball? It was the perfect time and place to attack. We should have known that!"

"Everyone needs to relax," Max said. "Even soldiers in a war need a break once in awhile. Otherwise you're just biding time until you mess up from exhaustion. You can't mess up, or you're dead."

"They're not relaxing," Graham yelled, pointing to the carnage back at the church. "They're getting stronger every damn day!"

"Hey! I get it!" Max wasn't going to back down. He flew into Graham's personal space. It was amazing how someone so small could instantly command such respect. An outsider might think to just slap the asshole like a fly, but to those of us who knew him, we understood he was not a pixie to underestimate. Graham backed up a step, but he didn't look ready to let himself or us off the hook. "I'm pissed, too. But it's done. It's over."

"Yeah? And now what, Max? Now what the hell do we do? They could walk into HQ right now and take it over if they wanted!"

"First of all, we shut the fuck up, right?" Max responded with an intensity that made Graham break eye contact with the boss man. "You want to scream something like that in the middle of the street? Really? Take a breath, kid."

"Sorry," Graham muttered. "I'm just..." He let out a breath. "What do we do now?"

"We find out who needs help. We lick our wounds. We come up with a plan."

Graham nodded.

Fay, sensing it was okay to help now, touched his shoulder. He pulled away and walked toward the church.

"What do we do about them?" I asked Max quietly. A small crowd was gathering around the church steps.

"Cleaners will take care of them, as usual. We just do our jobs."

"Got it," I said with a nod. I was grasping onto anything that made sense with the gusto of a lost child. "Okay."

I couldn't get my head around the disaster we'd just been through. I pushed a voice down as hard as I could, but I failed. It echoed in my head so hard that I couldn't see straight.

Chester is dead because of me.
Chester is dead because of me.

CHAPTER 9

The New York Paranormal Police Department HQ was usually a loud mess that was both my workplace and my apartment. My little room in the corner was a burden that I couldn't wait to escape.

I didn't like the place on a good day.

On a bad day, it was even worse.

Walking into the Main Room of HQ was unsettling. The hustle and din of working officers was barely a whisper. One look around and it was clear PPD was bare-bones, and that's a positive spin.

Really, we were in deep shit.

Bob and Lou walked in behind me. The goblins took one look around, grinned at each other and ran toward the maze of desks. They shuffled through drawers, peeked underneath papers and opened whatever wasn't locked down.

Bob laughed and held up something shiny.

"Yup! Spoon! Martinez skimmed some silverware from the Bronx assignment!"

"What an asshole," Lou replied. "Here it is. I knew it! Yee keeps his passwords on a piece of paper filed under 'Passwords'."

"What an asshole!"

I snapped my open mouth shut and tried to find the words to shut that bullshit down. "I only see two assholes at the moment," I called over to them. "What the hell are you two doing?"

"You kidding me, BB?" Bob yelled back in some twisted mockery of self-righteousness. "The place is empty, and Lou and I have about thirty bets going!"

When it came to money, games or bets, there was just no stopping New York goblins. They lost all sense of decency. What little decency they had, that is. Usually they could manage to hold onto a shred of it by the tips of their claws.

Bob and Lou met eyes and screamed "PORN!" at the same time. They ran to a desk and practically tore it to pieces.

Lou emerged from under a desk and raised something into the air. "USB KEY! TAPED UNDER THE SHELF!"

"PUT IT IN!"

"THAT'S WHAT SHE SAID!"

I'd had enough. The other officers' tired eyes started to follow my bodyguards around the room as they bounced from desk to desk. "Guys," I bellowed as I put a hand on each of their shoulders, "we lost officers tonight. You know that, right? We don't even know if the person at that desk is still alive."

That snapped them out of their frenzy long enough for them to look guilty. They stared at me with big, sad eyes. All the while, Lou tried to slip the USB key into the laptop behind him on the sly without looking. I shook my head. I needed to head to my room and get away from them. From everything.

"I knew it," Bob whispered excitedly. The goblins stuck their long noses into the screen. "Sanderson is a perv!"

"It's always the uptight ones," Lou giggled. "What's he... AAAAAAGH!"

"What is that?" Bob asked, pointing at the screen.

"I... have no idea," Lou said. He flicked the monitor off. I had to admit I was intrigued even as I walked away, but I was more intrigued by why Lou had such a reaction. What could possibly fluster that old goblin?

"Briefing Room," Max's voice said over HQ's speaker. "Now."

I did a U-turn.

No rest for the weary.

I counted twelve of us as we shuffled to the briefing room's door, including me. Thirteen, with Max.

Lucky thirteen.

"You okay?" I asked Fay as I sat next to her.

"I'll live," she said, staring ahead. "Not sure I want to at the moment, but—"

"Hey, don't talk like that unless you mean it," I said.

She broke her empty stare to look at me. My stomach dropped.

She was in bad shape. It was more than the disastrous night we'd just had. She'd been crying a lot recently as her mother, Cassandra, stepped into PPD business like an overprotective parent. I didn't know what to say. I remembered something Mike had told me when he was afraid of coming out. I wanted to be there for him, so I came up with a thousand ideas. Finally, he'd asked me to stop trying to solve his problems for him and just ask him one simple question.

"What can I do to help?" I asked Fay.

Her eyes immediately teared up, but she didn't get a chance to answer me because Max smacked his tiny hands on Sarge's podium to get our attention.

Typical pixie move.

He was so small, the only way he could get our attention was to freak us out.

"We're fucked," Max declared.

CHAPTER 10

"**G**reat leadership skills, partner," I pointed out before my brain could stop my tongue.

"Shut up, kid. We've been fucked before. Hell, we were fucked a few months ago. The attack a few months ago feels like ancient history because we made it ancient history. With willpower. With planning. We recruited like hell, and we got some excellent officers out of it."

"He's complimenting us?" Fay whispered to me.

"We really *are* fucked," I whispered back.

She giggled.

"Want to share what's so funny, Franklin?"

"Nothing, sir!"

"Maybe it's the dead PPD officers? You find that funny?"

"Hey, Max, come on," I broke in. "Lay off."

He shot me a frown. I mouthed, "Please." His brow relaxed, and he started flying around the front of the room, hands behind his back.

"The good news is that Sarge only suffered minor injuries. He'll be out of the hospital ward soon."

He cleared his throat. That was not a good sign.

"The bad news?" I asked for everyone.

Max sighed. "Nineteen officers are injured." We waited. The silence in the room was heavy with dread. We all knew there was more news to drop on our exhausted shoulders. "We lost three cops tonight."

The curses and gasps cut through the room and broke my heart.

"Martinez, King, and McLaughlin," Max managed to say with a cracking voice.

Again, the muffled sounds of grief flew through me. My stomach felt like a rock. I had to force myself to take a breath. The PPD had a lot of work to do, but we also had a lot of sadness to carry around while we did it. I didn't know any of the dead he'd mentioned very well, but I knew enough to know they were all good officers. Martinez was one of the few guys to smile at me when I'd first started at PPD. Fay had a crush on McLaughlin. I glanced over at her. She covered her mouth with her hand and did a good job of holding it together.

Max cleared his throat. "The other bad news is that twelve of the nineteen injured officers are in serious condition. Five are critical."

The noise that broke the room in two wasn't grief this time.

It was shock and surprise.

We all knew we'd taken a beating, but hearing a number that high just made it real.

"Zip it," Max yelled. "Shut up! You too, Simon." He

glared. "Yeah, like I said, it's bad. We're fucked." His look of resolve tightened. "So this is what we're gonna do. From what I can tell, most of you still have your partners here in the room with you. There's one stroke of luck, right?" That got a few mumbles. "Yee and Rogers, as you know, both of your partners are in serious condition. I need you to focus on your job and work together. Got it?"

The officers nodded, though worry and exhaustion were all over their faces.

"Not gonna sleep after all this," Yee mumbled. "So what do we do, Shakespeare? Point us in a direction."

Max took a seat on the podium's edge and leaned on his knees. He took the cigar out of his mouth, leaned back and tapped it out on Sarge's notebook. A few of us chuckled at that. We all hated that fucking notebook, but I could tell that my partner was stalling for time. He was making something up right then and there.

"The goblers are smarter and stronger than ever," he started. "The attack was well-coordinated." I made eye contact with Graham and said "Shut the fuck up" with sign language. We didn't need his doom-and-gloom opinion. He gave me the universal sign language of fuck you. "Graham and Black, zip it." I returned my attention to Max. "We're not going to sit around and wait for the mobgoblins to make another move. First up, we need to defend against an attack on HQ. We'll have three teams on defense. Three more teams need to track down the goblers that escaped tonight. Follow the fuckin' drool. Graham, I need you to track any activity tonight in known mob spots. Focus on ones that could be medical facilities. They've been known to hack into traffic lights to get around faster, so keep an eye on that. Chatter, too. Cell, net, landline."

"Smoke signals and pigeon?" Graham asked.

I could tell from his expression that he knew it was a mistake the second it came out of his mouth, but he didn't apologize. The chip on his shoulder was big enough to break his neck.

Max seethed, but held it in. Everyone knew he'd exact his punishment on the rookie in some sadistic way at a moment of his choosing.

Graham was usually a kiss-ass when it came to Max. I wondered what the hell was up with him.

Maybe it was the trauma of the evening?

I didn't have time to worry about it.

"Okay, teams," Max said, raising his voice to let us know it was time to stop talking and start doing, "arm up and work out team assignment and rotation on your own. I'm not your dad, so do things smart. We'll be thinking for ourselves, goddess help us." He shot Graham a sour look. "Dismissed. Good luck."

We all pushed our chairs back from the desks.

"Not you, Black. You stay."

Fay looked worried for me as she moved toward the door.

"Nuh-uh," Max added. "You too, Franklin. Sit."

CHAPTER 11

Fay and I were surrounded by scraping chairs and deep sighs as our fellow officers tried to muster enough hope to leave the room in one piece. Max had done as good a job as anyone to get them on their feet, but it was going to be tough to keep them moving forward. I don't think Sarge could have lit a bigger fire under our asses.

"Good job, partner," I said.

Max sat on the podium again with the grump face on. "Did I ask your opinion?"

"Did I deserve that response?"

He fished his cigar out of his vest pocket. "We're not going to have a hug-in, Black, if that's what you're looking for."

"Common decency and a basic understanding of how to interact with other living things would be great, thanks."

He smirked and lit his nasty cigar. "Nice. We need information."

His ability to change the subject, and his mood, was always a surprise to me. It was a New York trait, I think. I sighed and went along with his lighter tone. "What kind of information?"

"The kind that your mother might provide," Max said, looking at Fay.

Fay's eyebrows almost shot off her face in surprise. "My mom? What does she have to do with any of this?"

"She's an expert on weretigers, Franklin. You know that. She's helped Sarge since the whole gobler crap started, but he's out of the picture for now, and we need to get her take on what went down tonight."

"So you want us to pay Cassandra a visit," I stated. Out of all the things I thought he'd plan for me, that wasn't one of them.

"Mrs. Franklin, yeah," he replied, all courtesy all of a sudden.

Wait.

Did Max respect Cassandra?

"Hey, you're the one who told me to make friends with her," I shot back before I remembered Fay was sitting right next to me.

"Wait, what?" Fay glanced back and forth between the two of us. "Why do you want her to be friends with my mother?"

Max pursed his lips to stop himself from biting my head off. My track record of keeping secrets was getting worse every time I opened my mouth.

Max took a deep breath. "Because, rookie, your mother wants to be friends with Officer Black, that's why."

Fay crossed her arms. The thought of a visit to Cassandra wasn't going over well with her. "If you don't mind, I'll stay here with Graham and look for gobler and mob activity."

"I *do* mind. Yer going with Black."

Fay sighed and sunk in her chair. Nothing made her act like a teenager more than the thought of visiting her mother.

"What are you going to do?" I asked Max.

"Me? I'm gonna let Mrs. Franklin know yer coming. And then I get to be the boss for a few more hours. I'm going to take full advantage." Max winked at me and flew out of the room.

"What did he mean by that?" Fay asked.

I shrugged. "Could mean he's going to tap into the deepest, darkest secrets in confidential PPD files, and save our asses with a brilliant idea."

"Sounds smart."

"More likely, he's going to drink and smoke his cigars in the Main Room and do other things Sarge usually gives him shit about."

Fay smiled, even though I was being serious.

I stood up and took a deep breath. "You ready?"

"Nope," she grunted. "Let's go."

CHAPTER 12

*F*ay and I took a few minutes to get ourselves together.

I washed my face and took a quick look in the mirror. Nothing hanging out of my nose. Nothing between my teeth. Ready for the world.

It struck me that I was looking into the eyes of an officer who had lost a friend that night, but I felt separate from that officer. I felt like I couldn't look too deeply or I'd lose myself in her grief.

In my grief.

There wasn't any time for that.

The high windows of the PPD locker room glowed with the silver light of dawn. It was good to see the horrible night come to an end, but the new day also made the grief tougher to hold down.

I rubbed some gobler gunk off my 6er and slipped it into the holster, snapped it in nice and pat, and took a deep breath. It was time to face Creepy Cassandra again.

But I had one errand to run first.

69

I stepped from the locker room and eyed Sir Pickle's lab door on the other side of the huge Main Room. The door loomed large. I wasn't in the mood for a visit, but I couldn't speak to Cassandra without a visit to the vampire first.

Fay stepped into my line of sight. "You look like a statue. What are you staring at?"

"I need to speak with Pickle real quick," I said as I slipped past her. I realized after a few steps that Fay wasn't with me. "You want to come with?"

"Hell no," Fay rasped, punctuating it with a violent head shake. "That guy freaks me out. Did you see him at the bagel party Sarge threw?"

I rolled my eyes. "He's a good guy, Fay. You should get to know him. He's weird, but he's got a good head on his shoulders."

"Yeah, no."

"Fine. We'll take Junker. His snacks are with Pat."

Pat was the manager of the garage. The garage technician was a no-nonsense chick. Even Max knew better than to pull her into his bullshit. I envied her that.

"You and Junker have a spat?" Fay asked with a smirk. Junker was my car, for want of a better term. He had a mind of his own, and the appetite of a lion. "Why are the snacks with Pat?"

"Because the fucking car figured out how to reach his treats with those vines of his. He shoves them through the back seat's lining, pops the trunk and takes what he wants. So I started to store the bugs and worms and unmentionable things in the garage's office."

"Oh. I heard about that."

"Yeah, I thought it was a good idea, until Junker drove through the office walls for midnight snack number four."

"So now Pat carries them around. Smart."

"Junker knows better than to mess with her."

I knocked on Sir Pickle's door, as was my custom. I knew our resident vampire wouldn't answer, but I wanted to give him time to put away his vampire kink, or whatever he did in the confines of his undead man cave.

I opened the door and let out a small gasp. For the first time since I'd been in PPD, Sir Pickle's lab had its lights on. I felt like I was intruding on something. The door slammed shut behind me.

"Hello?" I called out.

No answer. I glanced over at the shelves with Sir Pickle's meticulously organized lab materials, evidence and loot.

One box in particular was the real reason for my visit.

I'd been drawn to the thing for weeks. The contents of that box were a mystery that had something to do with me, or with weretiger history.

With a deep breath, I took a step forward. I wasn't sure I wanted to know what was in that container. It had some kind of power over me. Something that made me lose self-control. I didn't need anymore of that.

"Hello, Bethany Black," Sir Pickle's voice said, oozing from the slightly ajar door at the end of the room. "Are you ready to open the box?"

"Nope."

"Ah," he replied. "Perhaps another time then?"

"I'm kidding, Sir Pickle. I'm not ready, but I'll do it

anyway. Where are you? Would you like me to turn the light off out here?"

"No, thank you. I'm trying to learn to tolerate it. Please join me in here."

The door at the back of the room slid open a little bit more, revealing a dark space with a dim orange glow. The orange slid over the floor like a spell of some kind and gave me a path to follow.

I entered the room, and the door slid shut gently behind me. I went half tiger and my eyes adjusted quickly to the darkness.

It was a simple room. One coffin sat in the corner with a nice coffin-side table. A pile of three books were perched on top of it. Vampires didn't actually sleep in coffins, except the weird ones, but that didn't stop my friend from doing it anyway.

A long work table against one wall was covered in an organized mess of glass tubes and unfamiliar tools.

In the middle of the mess was that box, with its beckoning contents.

Waiting for me.

Sir Pickle cleared his throat. "It's over th—"

"I see it." I didn't mean to be rude, but I was nervous.

I stood over the box.

It's hard to explain the effect it had on me. It drew me in like a pile of bacon is probably the best way to put it, considering what a bacon whore I am. I wanted to open it so badly and see what was inside. I also didn't want to have anything to do with it. There had been so many revelations in the last couple of weeks that I was getting exhausted from keeping it all in my head. Pickle had told me my blood results revealed I was over 100 years old. Cassandra outed herself as an expert in weretigers. And then there was the fact that something was building the gobler army faster than anyone expected.

And the only real explanation for that accelerated growth was that my claws, extracted from me when I was a babe, were probably being used by the mob to build their half-goblin, half-tiger army.

Whatever was in the box was not going to make my life easier. It was going to be another puzzle. Another clue to a mystery I couldn't even begin to get my head around.

"Would you like some help?" Sir Pickle asked from right behind me. I hadn't heard him approach me, so I jumped a little.

"No, Sir Pickle. I got it." I didn't really believe that, but I pushed the lid open.

I looked down at the necklace and I swear to the gods, the thing looked right back.

CHAPTER 13

*T*he necklace's decorative ornament sat face-up.

It was identical to the one I wore around my neck. The necklace that The Zoo told me my mother gave to me. It was a looping strand of thin metal coiled around itself like a snake ready to pounce.

I lifted it from the black velvet case lining and let it dangle in front of my half tiger eyes.

A deeper study showed it *wasn't* identical to mine.

Almost, but not quite.

The looping design was shined and buffed on one side. My necklace was buffed and shined on the other side. So, while they were the same shape, one of the necklaces flowed clockwise. The other one, mine, flowed counter-clockwise.

Sir Pickle walked beside me. His eyes were wide and filled with curiosity.

"Do you feel…" he whispered.

"Do I feel what?"

"…different?" he asked, blinking. It was a vague

JOHN P. LOGSDON & BEN ZACKHEIM

question from a vampire who was known for his directness.

I thought about it for a moment, then shook my head. "No. Should I?"

"I do not know, Bethany Black. The legacy of imbued materials carried through time by fate and grand design never broadcast intent, or narrative, beyond their implied importance."

I looked at him as I tried to process what he'd said. It was a mouthful and brainful, but I think I got the gist of it.

"Meaning you have no idea what it's supposed to do," I said with a comforting grin.

He released a small smile from its eternal prison. "Correct."

"And you don't know the story behind it, either?"

"Mostly correct."

I waited for him to continue, but he just stood there.

"Tell me what you know, Sir Pickle," I said with enough exasperation for even him to sense. Sometimes I could not figure that vampire out. He was an enigma one moment, and a good, helpful friend the next.

"The necklace was given to me by a mobgoblin boss years ago. Well, not given, per se."

"You stole it?"

"Steal is not a word I prefer to apply to this particular event. I was the mob's Scientific and Magic Officer, so he offered it to me for academic purposes. He wanted to know what it was, and if it could be used by the mobgoblins in their efforts to enrich themselves beyond all reasonable measurements until they each concluded upon their death beds that their lives had been for nothing, and their deaths would mean even less because of it."

"Oookay."

Sometimes you had to wait Sir Pickle out. He saw the big picture in the tiniest details, so he could meander a bit. I looked up at him until he got the hint that it was time to continue his explanation.

He poked through the contents of his worktable. I got the feeling he was searching for the best way to avoid eye contact with me.

"The mobgoblin was arrested and sent back to the Netherworld, leaving me to either inform the new mob boss that the necklace existed, or deny him that piece of information."

"So that you could use the necklace for your own purposes."

"Never, Bethany Black. I have no designs upon the world beyond the fleeting observations of truths. I took the necklace under my care."

"Again, you stole it," I noted, smirking.

He ignored me. "I spent years studying the relic. I never had much time to give it. Between the mob work and then switching over to PPD, things were...busy. But one day another item entered my purview in my duties as PPD lab technician and technologist."

"What kind of item?"

"I don't know, but it was delivered with an escort from the Netherworld in a refrigerated sleeve of Mylar, sealed airtight. I only got a glance at the bag as it was carried into my lab. I was ordered to mind my own business and to let the officers with the item in their possession go about their business. I was taken aback by the audacity of allowing strangers into my lab and then ordering me to tend to other business while said strangers partook of resources I'd spent years gathering, sometimes at great risk to myself."

"That is fucked up, yeah."

He nodded, satisfied enough with my outrage, succinct as it was.

"I wasn't going to leave my lab, though. Thus, I worked in this room here as they examined their object. After an hour of surrendering my space, I noticed a strong smell."

"Smell?"

"Yes, it's not only tigers who can smell well, Bethany Black. Vampires' sense of scent is nowhere near as powerful as yours, but many of us can pinpoint one smell better than any other. Perhaps because it's tied to our survival."

I knew what he meant, but it didn't make any sense.

"What are you saying, Sir Pickle?"

"I'm saying the necklace started to smell like blood. Just a hint at first, but the longer they stayed, the more intense the odor became."

I held the mysterious necklace up to my nose and sniffed. I sensed the sour smell of metal, but no blood.

Sir Pickle shook his head. "The smell is gone now. It disappeared the moment they took their project away from here."

"What were they working on?"

Again, he focused on his tidying up his worktable. "I don't know."

"But you suspect." He folded up some plastic baggies

and looked for a good spot to store them. "Sir Pickle? Don't go dark and mysterious on me. I'm here because you asked me to be."

That was a little disingenuous. He'd invited me to open the box, but it was my choice to do it, or not.

"I understand, Bethany Black. It's just that I'm afraid..."

He stopped himself from continuing again. I wanted to strangle him, but I opted for the patient path.

After a full minute of maddening silence, he had clearly made up his mind. It was time to tell me what the fuck was going on.

"I kept my ear to the ground, as I believe you people say. Once the strangers left my lab with their new knowledge, the odor of blood dissipated. I decided upon two paths. I'd take both paths at my leisure and follow them where they took me. First, I would work with Sue to gather as much information on the design of the necklace, the possible origins and the best resources to include in my quest."

I nodded. "That was a good plan."

"Not really. It was the second path that yielded the most fruit."

I knew Sir Pickle well enough to know he always took the most direct path forward when it came to his work. "You followed the technicians who soiled your lab?"

"Precisely."

"Very detective-like of you."

"Being around PPD has had its effects on me. I'm patient, but there was something about the situation that compelled me to act. With great haste."

His long pause meant he was either measuring his words, or he was recalling some details that stole his brain away from our discussion.

"Where did they go?"

"I followed the two men uptown to Rockefeller Center. They slipped into the subway. There's a shopping center underground that has a few dozen shops, restaurants, and one hundred and thirteen heavy brass doors."

"I think I remember them," I responded. "I visited Rockefeller Plaza when I first arrived in New York City. I wondered what was behind all of those doors."

"One hundred are service entrances, storage closets, and for other utilitarian uses."

"Where do the other thirteen go?"

Sir Pickle stopped fussing with his worktable and faced me. "It depends. They are open to the highest bidder. Some say they hold gold, other weapons, and some say there are portals there for smuggling."

"But you followed them through one of the doors," I more stated than asked.

"Yes. They showed the guard an ID, and they got in without a problem."

"How did you get in?"

"I...used all the tools at my disposal."

"Sir Pickle!"

"I didn't kill him, Bethany Black. I used the shadows to sneak up on him and...introduced him to sleep."

"Nice way to put it."

He quickly got back on track. Sir Pickle didn't suffer witty banter well. "I got downstairs just in time to see a door closing. I used every ounce of strength to get my foot lodged in before it shut. The door led to a set of metal steps to the subway below. Or a part of the subway. I've lived in this city for a very long time. I know the underground well, but I couldn't identify anything there. The architecture of the platform was older, with stacked stone for columns instead of tile. Brick floors perched over a set of tracks that shone like the brass doors above. I sniffed out the duo, but it was hard to tell which way they'd gone. There were only two choices. Left or right. I chose poorly."

"And you lost them."

He nodded. "The tunnel system in that area is a web. It's easy to lose someone tailing you, and even easier to lose your way. I ended up walking onto the F-Line tracks."

"I thought you said you made good progress by following them."

"I did," Sir Pickle said with no small amount of sass. "Please stand back, Bethany Black." I stepped back a few feet. "Further. All the way to the wall, if you would, please."

I leaned against the wall and crossed my arms, curious about what he was doing and annoyed that everything had to be so damn mysterious with him.

He lifted the edge of a floorboard up and flipped it over. Then he flipped the floorboard next to it. He moved a dozen planks on the floor, revealing an odd sight.

There were rows and rows of index cards filed in a line underfoot.

CHAPTER 14

*I*t was like a librarian had stowed his book catalogue under Sir Pickle's coffin room.

My friend poked his nose into one of the long rows of cards. He flipped through his records with the intense gaze of a librarian searching for the right resource for the millionth time. He pulled out a few slips of paper to check where he was in his search. I could see the browning paper, some covered in dark ink notes and others with paper clips weighing them down.

He pulled one out with more zest, and turned it around to study its backside. Then he glanced up at me, balanced himself on the thin space between the rows of index cards, and handed me the card.

The card had a photograph paper-clipped to it.

It was a picture of a man with black hair and dark eyes. The image was blurry, but I could tell he was handsome and confident. I could also tell he didn't know his picture was being taken.

I glanced up at Sir Pickle. "You took this picture while you tailed them?" He nodded. "Who is it?"

"I don't know. He held himself with a poise to match the Queen's butler, even while he eluded my formidable talent for hunting. I've explored the deepest records of topside and Netherworld for years, but there's no sign of him anywhere. Maybe you can find him, Bethany Black. If you do, you'll find someone with answers."

I studied the photo for a minute before slipping it into my jacket pocket. "Thanks, Sir Pickle. I'll see what I can do."

"I did learn that the two of them were considered specialists who worked closely with the PPD across the world," he offered. "They were usually assigned to top secret and sensitive cases."

"That would mean their bosses are familiar to the PPD."

"They may *be* the PPD, Bethany Black." He shook his head. "But the more I looked, the less I discovered."

"That's a sure sign someone knew you were onto them."

"Yes. That's what I thought as well, but the only people who knew of my quest were officers of the PPD."

"Implying the department really doesn't want you to know the truth."

"Some within the department, at least. It would appear so, yes. Even Sue…" He stopped himself from finishing his point.

I prodded him like a stubborn ox. "Even Sue, what?"

He frowned. "Even Sue was fed inaccurate information. It was subtle, but some of my questions about the necklace's design were answered with incorrect cultural attributions, and unfruitful contacts of expertise."

"Have you tried to track him down recently?" I asked, stealing another quick glance at the handsome man in the pic.

Sir Pickle's shoulders sunk a little bit. It was just enough body language for a cop who's getting good at her job to notice.

"No. I gave up."

"Don't look so down, buddy. We're all busy around here. I'll take over the chase."

"While I understand your motivations, Bethany Black, I feel as your friend that it is my duty to remind you, you're busier than all of us put together."

"I'm a rookie, vampire. I don't know any better." I winked at him so he knew I was playing around.

His mouth made something resembling a smile, but the expression probably would have terrified anyone who didn't know him.

I held the necklace up to the dim orange light and let it dangle next to my own necklace. They swung back and forth until they began to wrap around each other. For a second, I thought they were reaching for each other, but they'd been caught up in normal old gravity and physics. Nothing magic about it.

"Should I take it with me?" I asked.

He nodded.

I untangled the jewelry and slipped mine over my head first, and then the mysterious one next.

"Thank you for guiding me through this, Sir Pickle. I

know I can be a tough person to get along with." I gave him an encouraging smile. "You're a good friend."

"I fear you will change your mind as your quest continues."

That made me jolt slightly. "What makes you say that?"

"Everything. The goblers, the mobgoblins, the dead wizards, the slow disintegration of the New York Paranormal Police Department. It seems to me that everything is falling apart."

"Maybe that's the best time for everything to come together," I countered as he put the floorboards back in place. "We all have to choose sides. I've chosen the PPD. I know you have, too. When the time comes, we'll have as good a chance as the other guys to come out on top."

This time he did smile. It was real. There was nothing forced about it. It even showed in his eyes. I turned to leave, but when I reached the door, I stopped.

"Sir Pickle?"

"Yes?"

"What do you think those specialists had in that bag? What could be so top secret that they'd keep it from you?"

"I think you know the answer to that question, Bethany Black."

I did.

I didn't like it, but I knew the most likely answer was that they had my claws.

It was best to let it go unsaid, though, which I did as I slipped through the lab's door and closed it behind me.

I didn't know who was listening, after all.

CHAPTER 15

*M*y car, Junker, knew we were tired.

He had a special talent for turning a casual ride into a death-defying act, filled with exploding car parts, creepy backseat vines, and a pigheaded refusal to give up his steering wheel.

But the ride to Central Park was the most uneventful outing ever. The car was stubborn, but he was sensitive. He could tell we were tired, and not in the mood for his bullshit.

Junker idled as we got out, and even shut the doors behind us with his vines.

"What a gentleman," Fay cooed, smiling warmly. Junker let out a loud farting noise from his exhaust. "Or not." But she winked at the passenger's door.

Her smile disappeared as we faced the brownstone.

"Home, sweet home," she muttered, with an expression that said something more like, "Get me the hell out of here" and "What if I just blew the place up? Would that make my problems disappear?"

I put a hand on her shoulder and she smiled back, but there was no joy in that smile.

"Can I just run away?" she asked.

"We'll wait for Bob and Lou to arrive, and then we'll think about the best way to tackle this."

"You take her high and I'll take her low," she suggested.

I laughed, which broke the tension for about two milliseconds.

As I stood at the bottom step of the matriarch's Central Park domain, the last thing I wanted to do was talk to Cassandra.

In our previous meeting, we'd struggled our way through a creepy, manipulative, inappropriate twenty and a half minutes. Yeah, I had timed it. She hinted at knowing a lot about me and my kind, but made it clear she wouldn't share that knowledge with me unless I went along to get along. She'd tried to get me to spy on her own daughter and conspire against her. Cassandra clearly didn't want Fay in the PPD. Or she thought Fay wasn't fit to be an officer, which was bullshit. But it was the testing that pissed me off. She'd challenged me and my skills in her weird underground lab where she was holding Jonny, the first goblin to be changed into a tiger. He'd been recovering from the process in some kind of tube of green liquid.

If he was recovering at all.

I suspected Cassandra was doing more than just treating Jonny. I couldn't get over the vision of him waking up during my visit to the lab. He had looked at me like he wanted help.

As I stood there, examining the brownstone's front

door as if it were the path to hell, I wondered if she was experimenting on the poor mobgoblin.

"BB?" Lou asked from beside me. "You okay?"

I jumped slightly, and then nodded. "Yeah, fine. Didn't hear you arrive. Welcome to the party." I glanced over at Fay, whose expression was probably identical to the one I'd just shaken away. "You okay, Fay?"

"I'll be fine, Bethany," she said. She suddenly had a distant tone to her voice. I knew that tone well. It appeared whenever she remembered she was mad at me. Max and I had manipulated her and Graham during the Club 1 disturbance. My partner had pretended to be a double-crossing cop, and I'd gone along with him against my better judgment.

I led the way, with my goblin bodyguards and Fay behind me. I did a double-take when I realized Graham was taking up the rear. He'd ridden with my bodyguards. I didn't know why he'd joined us, since he was supposed to be working his research magic for Max. I almost asked him to explain himself when the front door opened.

I glanced up at Cassandra. She was comfortable on her perch, standing above everyone else. It was her natural way of being. She was probably born on a fucking pedestal and just dropped into the doc's arms.

"Welcome, officers," she said. The way she said 'officers' may as well have been 'children'. "Please, come in. I have snacks in the sitting room."

We all entered without a word.

Cassandra didn't require us to talk and I didn't feel like, "Fuck you, bitch," was a good way to start our little visit.

We filed into the same room where she'd grilled me on the last visit. The coffee table was covered in New York's finest victuals. Bagels and lox. Muffins. Scones. Piping hot coffee. It looked and smelled scrumptious. I would have loved to dive in, mouth first, but that would give her the advantage.

Graham didn't see things the same way, apparently.

He scooped up one of everything in a mad dash for carbs and caffeine that only a true snack addict could pull off.

"Dig in, young man," Cassandra said with a satisfied grin.

"He can't hear you, mother," Fay informed.

Cassandra smiled and pointed at Graham. "Oh, is this the deaf boy?"

"He's a man," Fay shot back. "An officer. He *can* read lips, so just make sure he's looking at you when you say anything he should hear."

"That's fine, dear."

Oh crap, it was going to be hard to keep my claws out of this woman's butt.

My goblin bodyguards tore into the muffins so hard that crumbs were flying all over the room. Cassandra watched them make a mess of her place, but she didn't seem to mind. She observed the chaos as if she knew all along that the PPD would act like this when visiting her home.

"Are you two done?" I asked Bob and Lou as they sat on the floor with two loud thumps and burped in harmony. Bob tried to get up to snag some more carbs but he fell back down on his rump.

"Looks like it, yup," he groaned.

"I would have had donuts from Eddie's if you'd given me a little more preparation time," Cassandra noted.

She took a seat like a queen would take a throne. She even turned her knees to the side and placed both arms on the armrests, hands draped over the edges.

I cleared my throat and forced out some polite words. "It's fine, Mrs. Franklin. It's kind of you to go to the trouble."

She shot me a frown straight out of *Grandma's Book of Scaring Guests to Death*.

"Do we really need to go through this again?"

I sighed, remembering a little detail from our last conversation.

"Thank you, Cassandra," I amended. She wanted us to be on a first-name basis, and Max wanted me to get along with her, so I swallowed my pride. "We'd like to talk to you about something that happened last night."

"The attack at the ball," she replied. "What a tragedy."

The rest of us shot each other glances. I was the first to ask, "How did you know about that?"

"Know about it?" She took a slow sip from her teacup, which was not big enough to cover her smirk. I think she enjoyed our surprised expressions. "I was there, dear."

CHAPTER 16

"*W*hat?" Fay asked. Loudly.

"Yes. I was there. I *paid* for the silly thing."

"I didn't see you," I said.

Cassandra's smirk faded and she shifted her crossed legs. "I was on the balcony when they broke through the windows. Horrible."

I was getting pretty good at reading people, and my read was that she was being honest. It may have been the first time I'd ever experienced that with her. I took some comfort in the fact that she was able to show some small amount of humanity.

"Tell us what you saw," Graham said, somehow. The bagel in his mouth was fighting for more molar time.

"I saw what you saw," Cassandra replied. "Those horrible creatures crashed the party and attacked you and your fellow officers."

"But not you," Fay accused.

"Hmmm?" her mother hummed. The muscles on her

face tensed. She'd switched to matriarch mode in a split second.

"You weren't attacked, Mother."

Cassandra put the tea cup on the side table. "You sound disappointed."

Fay didn't reply, but she had made a great point.

"If you were on the balcony then you would have been in the line of fire," I pointed out.

Cassandra let the silence linger for a couple of seconds. She calmly set her hands on her lap and wrapped her fingers together. "Am I being interrogated in my own home?"

I needed to damp down the heat a bit. "Cassandra, we're here to get a better picture of what happened last night, and how we can stop it from happening again. It sounds like you were in a position to see things we couldn't."

Cassandra slid her eyes away from her seething daughter and onto me. "Like I said, Bethany, I saw them attack some officers before Pedro pulled me outside."

"Pedro?" Graham asked.

Lou nodded. "She means Sarge."

Graham squinted and cocked his head. "Sarge's real name is Pedro?"

"Pedro Jonathan Ortiz McCallister," Bob half-said, half-burped. "Bronx born and raised."

"I didn't know you had a history with Sarge," I said. I knew it was off-topic, but gossip has a way of derailing the moment, no matter how heavy.

Bob brought another muffin down to his mouth and

waved it over his lips as if he was measuring the odds of stomaching another bite.

"He arrested us a few times when we were younger."

Lou grabbed the muffin and threw it back on the plate, adding, "He was such a dick."

"So were we." Bob grabbed the muffin again and stuffed half of it in his mouth. He gave Lou a defiant look and jerked like he might barf.

I turned back to our hostess. "So Sarge...Pedro was your date?"

"No, we're old friends. He was telling me what a good job Fay was doing before those ghastly things attacked." She smiled at her daughter who glanced around for an escape hatch. "Is Pedro okay? I heard he'd been injured."

"He should be out of the ward today," I said.

She leaned back in her chair. "Oh, thank the gods."

I sat across from Cassandra and leaned my elbows on my knees. "You're an expert in weretigers. What do you make of the goblers from last night?"

Cassandra sighed. "They're much further along than I thought they'd be, frankly. Your friend down in the lab is a caveman compared to them."

I nodded. "Jonny, yeah. You were afraid they'd get more advanced. But how can there be so many of them? All from one claw?"

That made her uncomfortable. I didn't like the pause. It meant she was getting ready to lie her ass off.

"Don't lie," I said, directly.

I'm not sure how my brain let that escape my mouth, but I'm glad I did. Her guilty face relaxed as she decided to come clean.

Or, at least, as clean as Cassandra could get.

She shook her head. "There's no way they built an army of those monsters with one claw."

Her eyes wandered away from meeting mine. I bent forward a little so she couldn't avoid me. "Then you're saying that they've either found a way to reproduce the spell without claws—"

"Or there are more claws out there," Bob finished for me.

"I want to know where they got those claws," I said.

Cassandra frowned. "I think you know the answer to that, Bethany."

"I want to hear you say it," I said, standing.

She looked up at me, her lips lifting into a smirk to end all smirks. "Will that make it more true, or less true?"

"No more games. Tell me, Mrs. Franklin."

She sighed. "Here we are back on a formal name basis, Officer Black."

I stepped toward her. "It's better than calling you what I really want to call you."

"BB," Fay said in a tone that suggested I get hold of myself.

"No, it's fine, Fay," Cassandra said with a fake smirk on her face. "I have this effect on people at times."

"I'll ask again. Where are the other claws coming from?"

"From you, I'm afraid."

It was one thing to theorize I was the source of the gobler army. It was another thing to face the truth. My face ran hot. "Are you afraid, Cassandra?" I asked. "Because if you ask me, you're not afraid of much."

"BB," Graham said in a calm voice.

"Oh my, how interesting," Cassandra said. Fay glanced at me, and gasped. Lou quickly stepped between me and our hostess. But Cassandra peeked around his shoulder and asked me, "Do you usually partially transform when you lose your temper, Officer Black?"

Shit.

CHAPTER 17

I glanced down at my hands.

Or should I say, paws?

I fell into a chair. I was able to sit upright, so my body must have been mostly human. I willed myself to transform back. It wasn't easy. For a split second, I wondered if I'd be able to pull it off.

My eyes met Lou's. He nodded. "Yer back to human, sweetheart."

"But you're as red as a beet," Cassandra said with a little too much curiosity in her tone of voice. She was studying the moment like a scientist.

The room was silent. I felt like my pants had fallen down. I was proud of my tiger form, but not being able to control it? That was humiliating.

"You call this being a good host, mother?" Fay asked. She took two big steps toward Cassandra. "You make all of us feel uncomfortable and insult PPD police officers?"

Cassandra put a hand on Fay's shoulder. "Fay, dear, I don't think…"

JOHN P. LOGSDON & BEN ZACKHEIM

Fay pushed her hand away. "You should be ashamed of yourself! I wouldn't blame them for leaving here right now."

"It's okay, Fay," I said.

"No, it's not okay, Bethany. My mother prides herself on being one of Manhattan's finest hostesses and she's acting like an amateur."

"Oh dear, I am so sorry," Cassandra breathed. I thought she was being sarcastic at first, but her pale skin and unblinking eyes convinced me otherwise. "Fay, you're correct. I don't...I don't know what came over me. I'm so sorry everyone. Please accept my apology. All of you."

I didn't know if she was ordering us, or imploring us, but her face showed me that she was being as honest and real as I'd ever seen her.

I leaned forward, elbows perched on my knees. I was tired. Actually, I was more exhausted than I'd ever felt before.

Graham and Fay sat down in the chairs on either side of me. Fay put a warm, calming hand on my back. "You never talk about your missing claws, BB," she said. "Who took them?"

"Yeah," Graham said. "If we find out who took them, then we find their supplier."

"I don't know," I replied. "Cassandra?"

Our hostess sat back down in her large chair. Her demeanor was different. She was more present. More ready to talk, maybe. "I don't have any answers for you, Bethany. The official story is all I know. One morning you had the claws, the next day you did not."

"How can I believe that you know nothing, when you keep showing off how much you know?" I asked. "You don't strike me as someone out of the loop when it comes to weretigers."

She sighed. "Yes. That would usually be true. But I only got involved with your care after the claws disappeared."

Fay and I glanced at each other. Neither of us believed her.

"What did you do to get involved, exactly?" Fay asked.

Cassandra frowned. "Well, first of all, I marched into The Zoo and used my influence to make some changes."

"What changes?" Graham asked.

"I pulled some strings and found a new Director for The Zoo."

"Damn," Graham said for all of us. The level of Cassandra's influence suddenly crystallized in that moment.

Cassandra shot him a frown. "Now, now, young man," she scolded, as if his language was more distasteful than what she'd just said.

"Sorry," he responded, meekly.

"You got Director Camp her position at The Zoo?"

Cassandra nodded. "She's a fine leader. A good mind and a steady hand at the helm. She was just what The Zoo needed. I'd go as far to say that she was just what you and your fellow weretiger needed, Officer Black. I'd also say that if you want answers then you need to go talk to Director Camp directly."

Cassandra was passing the buck. She was squirming free of answering my questions like the pro she was.

But I was done waiting. I was done playing games. I needed to know who had my claws.

I had the photo.

I had the desperation.

The element of surprise was on my side, if I chose to leverage it.

My temper took over and, once again, made a bad decision for me.

I pulled the photograph out of its folder, and held it up for Cassandra to see. Everyone else in the room angled themselves and moved into position to see what I was showing her.

"Who is this?" I asked Cassandra.

I was hoping the mystery man in the photo would be familiar to her. If the subject was a player on her level of politics then it was likely she'd be able to ID him.

But I didn't expect the response I got.

"Where did you get that?" Cassandra asked me, voice quivering. "When was it taken?"

I tried to keep my poise, but there was something about the way her voice shook that made me uneasy. "Answer my question," I said, trying to hold my ground. "I think this man knows who took my claws. He may be able to help us find them."

"Bethany," Fay said, meekly.

"What, Fay?" I asked, not taking my eyes off of her mother. Cassandra's face had settled into a mask of anger and confusion.

Fay took the picture from my hand, put it back in its folder, and handed it back to me. "You may want to coordinate with us the next time you have evidence."

My stomach dropped.

"What's wrong?" I asked.

Fay's sad eyes met mine. "That's my father."

CHAPTER 18

*T*he silence was like a vacuum, waiting to be filled by whoever had the guts to step up.

My big gamble hadn't paid off. I'd never asked about Fay's father. I'd assumed he was either dead or divorced from Cassandra.

"I didn't..." The sting across my face stopped my words cold.

Cassandra had slapped me.

Her eyes bored a hole in my head. "How dare you come in here and wave his photo around!" She pointed at the photo, which had fallen to the ground.

"I'm sorry," I said as loudly as I could through the pain. But my words didn't have any effect on the rage in that room.

If Cassandra's head had been on straight, I'm sure she could have found a way out of her bind. The way her stare wouldn't break from mine, though, made it clear I'd touched on something big.

"I'll go," I announced.

I stole a glance over my shoulder. Fay's eyes were filled with questions I knew I wouldn't be able to answer. I'd gone to the apartment to find answers of my own, but all I'd found was a fucking mess.

"BB, wait!" Lou yelled.

I stumbled from the brownstone and leaned against the stair's rail. I half-walked, half-slid to the sidewalk below. Junker let out a loud vroom that sounded like a combination of a 'hello' and 'what the hell is going on?'

I dropped my right hand from my cheek. Cassandra had left a hell of a cut with her fingernail. It stung like hell, but there wasn't much blood on my palm.

I hopped into Junker. The vines from the back seat curled toward me and slithered over the headrest. They gently settled on my cheek. I pushed them off.

"I'm fine, Junker."

The vines kept trying to get around my defenses. I slapped at them angrily, but Junker wouldn't stop reaching for the wound. I sighed and let the anger go. It had gotten me in enough trouble that day.

The vines covered my cheek. Within seconds, the cut stopped hurting.

I sighed with relief. "You're full of surprises, aren't you?" I asked the car. He was silent for once. I heard the vines make a wet noise. They were regurgitating some kind of salve onto my cut.

Max would want me to check in with him. Cassandra definitely wielded some useful information. At great cost to my flesh, of course.

But I wasn't ready to loop him in yet. If I told him

Director Camp was next on my list of interviews, I'd get intense pushback.

The drive to HQ was a haze. My crowded brain didn't know what to focus on. I pulled up to the PPD building and did my best to ignore the comic store front. Chester had worked there. He'd done a masterful job of keeping up the PPD front. We'd stayed hidden from the wrong people, and non-people, thanks to him.

Now the storefront was just a reminder of my lost friend. My failure.

I got ready to step into the portal to the Netherworld when someone cleared their throat from behind me.

I knew that throat-clearing sound all too well. I'd grown up with it. I closed my eyes. I just couldn't escape the boys.

"I need to do this alone, Lou," I said without turning around.

"No can do, BB," Lou said.

"You know better, hon," Bob added. "We're always right behind you."

"Okay, Bob," Lou cut in. "No need to get creepy about it."

"What! It's true! We're standin' behind her right now!"

I turned and took a big, angry step toward them. They backed up a few feet, but they didn't take their eyes off of mine.

I lost the staring contest.

"Fine," I said. "But you do what I say. This is PPD business. I'm the boss. Don't second-guess me. Don't make your own plans. Don't make hand gestures behind my back while I'm talking to someone."

Bob crossed his arms. "Can we breathe?" he asked, with lemon-powered sourness.

"Not if it's one of your 'Sighs That Speak a Thousand Words', Bob, no."

Lou turned to his seething cousin. "So we can breathe in, but we can't breathe out."

"Good idea," I said as I turned and stepped away from New York City.

CHAPTER 19

I should have prepared myself for my first visit back.

It had been months since I'd been to the Netherworld. I guess I thought it would feel natural, like returning home. But it freaked me out. It freaked me out so much that I went half tiger.

"What the fuck, BB?" Lou asked. "You smell trouble?"

I took a deep breath and changed back to human. I didn't want to make a big deal out of it, so I just muttered, "Sorry."

Of course, this was Bob and Lou, so trying to put an end to a conversation was like trying to eat an ice cream cone in an oven.

Bob ran ahead of me as we started the short trip to The Zoo. He walked backwards, wearing his concerned expression. I wanted to bop him on the nose. "You just went half tiger, sweetheart!"

"I'm aware of that, Bob."

He threw his arms up. "Why did you do that?"

"To freak you out."

Bob turned to walk beside Lou. The two of them stared up at me like I owed them money.

I rolled my eyes. "Guys. Drop it."

Bob did his best to keep up with me as I lengthened my stride. "This is the second time in the last hour. Has this been happening a lot?"

"No." I felt bad about lying but I'd do anything to focus on the job ahead of me.

It was Lou's turn to jump into the action. "How long have you been changing without meaning to?"

"Since your mother…" I stopped myself. I wasn't going to lose my shit. I felt the weight of being in the Netherworld. I didn't know why I was so nervous until The Zoo came into view.

Then it hit me.

The oxygen in my body was pulled out through my nose. All I had was a beating heart and lungs that forgot how to work right.

It wasn't the Netherworld that had me freaked out. It was my old home. My old prison.

"Grab her!" Lou yelled. He and Bob reached up and held me on my feet. I would have fallen on my face if they hadn't been there.

They sat me down on a bench and hovered over me.

Lou got in my face. "BB, you okay?" I found enough breath somewhere in my body to nod. "Come on, BB. Talk to us. What's going on?"

Bob smacked his cousin on the back of the head. "Isn't it obvious, you moron?"

"No, it's not obvious, ya pickle knub!"

"Oh, that's a new one! Where did you get 'pickle knub'?"

"I made it up, ya moist chubbyhole."

"Ian Dex's crew," Bob mumbled. He leaned toward me and whispered. "He got this shit from someone on the Vegas crew."

"And what if I did? Steal from the best, I say. Can we get back to BB now? Is that okay with you, Bob?"

"No, we can stick with you," I told him, hoping to avoid the goblin third-degree, which can feel like something between an enema and water torture.

"She's anxious about going back to The Zoo, Lou," Bob said. "She just had a panic attack or somethin'."

Lou threw his arms in the air. "Well, why didn't you say so?"

"How long, BB?" Bob asked, getting back to business with his annoying Serious Face.

I gave up. "A couple of months now. Not sure what's going on."

"Stress maybe," Lou suggested. "Adrenaline kicks in and boom, you get tiger-y."

I shrugged. I had my breath back. The cold sweat covering my body was uncomfortable, but it helped to ground me. "Maybe. I'm fine now. We need to get going. I want this visit over with."

All three of us looked up at The Zoo's main entrance. It was a nondescript building, except for the sheer size of it. Dozens of windows looked out on the street. I spotted my old room and felt the panic rise again.

Bob patted me on the back and saved me from another wave of panic.

My goblin bodyguards bickered over who would push the call button on the front door. I stepped in and did it myself.

They glanced up at me, concerned.

I looked inside myself. I was concerned, too.

CHAPTER 20

*T*he smell of the place flowed over me.

I managed to take a deep breath and my whole body settled down.

I could do this.

I was a PPD officer now. I'd proven myself to everyone in that place. If anyone should be having a panic attack, it was Director Camp.

"Hey, Bitty!" a deep voice called out from down one of the four hallways that branched off of the reception area. Big Johnson, a troll friend of mine, smiled and waved. 'Bitty' was Big Johnson's nickname for me. He'd grown up in The Zoo, too. The last surviving member of a tribe of shamans. He'd become the janitor, but I always got the sense there was much more to him than zoo maintenance.

As he walked toward us, the tiled floor vibrated slightly. A big part of his job was fixing the damage he did to the place by just existing.

"Hi, Big Johnson," I said, as I gave him a hug.

He was just the right guy to ground me again. He'd always been an ally in my grudge against The Zoo.

He gently clutched my shoulders, and held me at arm's length like a proud uncle. "You've been doing well, I hear."

"Yeah? What have you heard?"

"Just that you're a born officer. You have a few notches in your resume now."

I smiled. "If you mean cuts and bruises, then that's true."

The troll glanced down at my tails. "Bob, Lou," he said with a slight nod.

"Big guy," they said together with their own little nods.

Big Johnson turned his big eyes back to me. Troll eyes can be terrifying things. But my friend's brow softened and I felt his affection wash over me. "It's what you wanted, right, Bitty? The job?"

I nodded. "It is, Big J." I don't know why, but I felt like having a big, messy sobfest. I had to stop that from happening, so I changed the subject. "How's The Zoo?"

His head jerked back and he busted out a bellowing laugh. "As if you care!"

"I care!" I said, way too defensively. "Right guys?"

The boys looked away.

So much for them having my back.

Big Johnson shrugged. "It's a mess, as usual. It keeps me busy. They just brought in a couple of troll orphans from Peru. They like to tear the place up for shits and giggles. Nothing I can't handle."

Something he'd said earlier suddenly hit me. "Wait. Who told you I was a born officer?"

"Director Camp."

"Get the fuck outta here," I said with my best New York accent. It was actually pretty damn good, if I do say so myself.

He smiled back and patted me on the shoulder.

"She's a fan, Bethany. Don't let her tough exterior fool you."

A new voice broke into the conversation. "Is the plan to keep me waiting for much longer? Because I have a busy schedule."

I knew who it was before I turned.

Director Camp waddled down another hallway, toward reception. Her short, stocky body was deceptive. It made her look like a box with a face that only a drunk and partially blind mother could love. I'd seen her move like a tiger when she dodged an attacking werewolf a few years back, though. She might have been a goblin, but she had a special talent for dodging more than just the politics of running The Zoo.

The director pulled the cigar from between her teeth and knocked some ash off the tip and into Big Johnson's rolling trash receptacle.

I put on my polite voice. "Hello, Director Camp."

"Bethany," she muttered with a slight nod of the head. "So, what the hell do you want?"

"Right to the point, as usual."

"You think you leave and everything changes?" She gave me a look, before taking a hit from her cigar. "What do you want, girl?"

"Officer," I shot back.

She smirked, chewing on the tip of the cigar. Then, she nodded to the point of almost bowing. "Officer."

I glanced at the boys, then back at her. "We need to talk in private. It's PPD business."

"Figured as much." She glanced over at my guards. "You two coming along to protect her?"

"That depends," Bob replied. "Will she need protecting?"

Camp shot me a frown. "That depends on how cheeky her new authority makes her."

Lou stepped between the two of us. "Then yeah, we're coming with her."

I wasn't sure if he'd come to that decision because he didn't trust me and my temper, or because he thought Camp was an actual threat. The end result was the same. All four of us walked down the familiar hallways toward her office.

I told myself I was ready for this about 100 times before we walked into her domain.

I was wrong.

CHAPTER 21

"*Y*ou know about the mess we're dealing with topside," I said before she could take a seat at her way-too-big desk.

It wasn't a question, and Camp knew it. She nodded and pushed the cigar box toward us. Bob and Lou both snatched one with way too much enthusiasm.

Then Lou took a second cigar, sheepishly, and slipped it into his pocket. Camp rolled her eyes.

"What?" Lou said. "I like these. They don't make 'em like this up there."

Camp sighed. "Fine, Lou. Take whatever you want. You deserve it, watching over this one." She gestured a thumb in my general direction.

I crossed my arms to keep my hands from pounding the desk. "Do you really need to push my buttons before I get started?"

"We're jockeying for position here, girl." She held up her hands in surrender. "Excuse me... *Officer*. We've got to see who starts the meeting with the upper hand."

117

I reached into my pocket, pulled out my hand, and slapped it onto her desk.

Everyone looked at my hand for a few seconds.

"Oh, it's an invisible thing," Lou said, innocently.

"No, it's not an invisible thing," I said without taking my eyes from the Director.

"There's nothing there, Officer Black," Camp said, squinting up at me.

"Exactly, and that's the problem." They were all frowning at me. "My claws, Director Camp. They're missing."

"Ooooo," Bob said, chuckling.

"Clever, BB!" Lou added.

I growled. I couldn't help it. They were doing exactly what I warned them about. I didn't need them distracting me.

"I think it may be better if you two waited outside, after all," I said, pointing at the door.

"Shit!" Bob yelled. "We just stepped on her moment."

Lou threw his hands up. "We? You're the one who stepped on her moment. I didn't say anything until you said something."

"Out!" Camp and I yelled together.

The goblins collected themselves and tried to leave with some dignity.

"We're right outside if you need us, BB," Bob said. He stuck his chest out and shot Camp a frown to save some face.

"Thank you, Bob," I replied with as much courtesy as I could muster.

I waited until they closed the door. Then I waited five seconds longer.

Bringing my finger up to my lips, I carefully got up from my chair and walked over to the door. I yanked it open and the goblins almost fell over from the weight of pressing their ears to the wood.

"Out!" I yelled. "Go steal some food from the cafeteria or something!"

I watched them sprint down the long hall before I closed the door once again.

With that, I spun back and looked at Director Camp.

"Where are my claws?"

"How the hell should I know?"

"You're the Director of The Zoo. You had custody of me when they were removed."

"That was before my time."

"I see," I said. "So, you're telling me that you took on your new job and didn't ask any questions about the clawless weretiger down the hall?"

She regarded me for a few seconds, her eyes squinting due to the smoke tickling them from the cigar. She took another hit and tapped the ashes into a tray before answering my question.

"I asked questions, sure," Camp said, chewing on her lower lip for a second. "I didn't get answers, but that's to be expected. My focus was on keeping you healthy and happy. Managed to do the former, but that whole happiness thing was elusive."

"I wonder why that would be. Maybe it had something to do with the fact that I was kept here against my will?"

"Oh, bullshit. You were kept here to make sure you were safe. You could have left at any time with the right reason. That reason just didn't come up until the PPD needed you."

"Really? Maybe you could explain all the times you let Mike run off to New York City to model while you rejected my requests to visit any of the PPD offices?"

"I had my reasons," she replied, but her voice wasn't quite as strong as before.

"And I deserve to know what they were."

The silence in the room gave way to a screaming voice in my head as I yelled at myself. Why the hell was I talking about personal business? I needed to focus on the claws.

Just the claws.

And, as if she'd read my mind, Camp asked, "Is this why you came down here, Black? I thought you had PPD business."

I tried to compose myself. "It's all getting mixed up, if you didn't notice."

"Yeah, I noticed that *you're* mixing it up. That doesn't mean the rest of us need to get pulled into your business."

That was rich. Here sat the woman who held the keys to every room in The Zoo. She knew what was going on day in and day out. She could damn well predict the mental climate of every animal...*prisoner* in the place.

For her to claim any level of innocence was asinine.

"You've made your career out of being in other people's business, Director," I said, almost wishing I'd had a cigar to flick the ashes off of for dramatic effect, "so you'll forgive me if I take that with a grain of salt."

That was a little too personal. I could tell she was pissed. She took another puff of her cigar, leaned forward and smashed the embers in her ashtray. "You want to know why I never let you visit the PPD?" I let my glare answer her question. She sat back in her leather office chair slowly. "They didn't want you there."

You know that feeling you get when you hear bad news? Not just bad news, but awful and unexpected news. That burn of grief, shock, anger—it can burn a hole in your head. When it travels to your gut, you feel sick. You could give in and throw it up, or you could push it down, let it linger until your muscles find a way to relax.

I managed to push it down, but just barely.

"I told you you wouldn't like it, Black," the Director said.

I resumed my seat and tried to hide my anger and disappointment. I filtered through my brain for all of my questions and found one.

"Why?"

"Why did they not want you? Hell if I know. They took you in the end. That's all that counts, right?" She sighed. "Look, Black...*Bethany*. PPD is law enforcement, intelligence, politics. If you have all of that piled up into one organization, it's enough to sap the life out of everyone. I admire your commitment to it. I do. But you have to step back and see it for what it is."

"A job, you mean."

"I was going to say it's a snake pit, but a job is a good way to look at it, I guess. It's dangerous in the best of times. But when it's under attack? Deadly. Power vacuums, jockeying for resources, selfish priorities." She laughed in a not-so-funny way. "Fucking mess. I didn't want you mixed up in that crap. I was glad they showed no interest in you."

"Then why did they change their mind?"

"No idea."

"Okay," I continued, using what I'd learned from watching Max question bad guys over the months, "then who asked for me to join up?"

She broke her eye contact with me. The pause lasted too long. I'd reached the end of my patience when she reached for her cigar box.

"I asked—"

Camp cut me off. "I heard you, Officer Black." She then caught herself and slumped slightly, letting out a long breath. Finally, she looked up at me. "Shakespeare asked for you."

I started to think maybe this trip was a mistake. I wiped my face and tried to take in the news.

It didn't make sense.

"But Max wanted nothing to do with me. We ended up partners because Sarge assigned us."

When I'd been assigned to Max, I'd just come off of a disastrous debut that ended with an officer in the hospital ward because of my actions. I thought I'd be kicked out. So it was a big surprise when I was partnered with the most experienced and talented officer in the NY PPD.

It was my turn to lean back in my chair. I hit the back of it so hard, I almost lost my balance.

I'd come down to The Zoo to find out more about what happened to my claws years ago. Instead, I was getting blasted with information that threw me off my game.

"Anyway," I said, "thanks for telling me." There was obviously going to be a discussion had between me and my partner. For now, though, it was time to get back to business. "Are there records of my arrival at The Zoo?"

"Of course. You want to see them?"

"Yes, please."

Camp leaned forward and put her chin in her hands, chewing on the cigar the entire time. "Get a warrant."

"You're kidding me," I scoffed.

"Nope." She shook her head, "Sorry, but I can't give them to you in your capacity as an officer without a warrant."

"Then give them to me in my capacity as the fucking subject of said records!"

"I could have done that if this was a social visit," she said, "but you've made it clear this meeting is part of your job as an officer of the New York Paranormal Police Department." She leaned in a little further. "You don't really have jurisdiction in the Netherworld, but seeing that you've been allowed to visit tells me that the Netherworld PPD has your back on whatever it is you're looking for." They didn't, but she wasn't aware of that. "So, that makes your request an official one, not one that's coming from a person who was a prior resident."

"You're going to split hairs with me?"

"Hair-splitting is in the job description, so yes."

I was so pissed, I looked around the room for something to arrest her for, even though the charges would be dropped immediately. She was right. Netherworld PPD hadn't sanctioned this visit. Still, if she wanted to play that game, then I'd play it.

My eyes stopped on her face and my rage died in an instant.

"I'm sorry," she said.

And she *did* look sorry.

So much so that I was immediately willing to believe her.

She had done a Jekyll and Hyde kind of thing, but I kind of understood that. She was protecting me, the patient, from me, the officer. It was fucked up, but it also made a warped brand of sense.

Besides, I couldn't handle any more drama.

Her revelation that I wasn't wanted by PPD, and that Max made a special request for me, was already enough to fill up my brain.

As I sat in that office with the woman I'd always considered my warden, I wanted to say a hundred things.

I wanted to scream hundreds more.

Instead, I stood, turned my back on her, and I walked out of there as fast as I could.

CHAPTER 22

J'd never been in a courtroom before. After two seconds in one, I didn't want to be in one ever again.

It felt like walking into a sauna. The intense heat and heavy silence was coupled with two men staring at me: the judge and the courtroom guard.

I walked the long carpet to the dais.

"Officer Bethany Black," the guard mumbled. "New York Paranormal Police Department. State your badge number for the records, please."

"Badge number 09055."

"Proceed," the guard said.

I moved up to the main podium. It was unnerving, to say the least. I couldn't even imagine what it would feel like to be the focus of a crime in here.

"Your honor," I said, trying to manage a small smile.

"Hmph," he grunted.

"Thank you for seeing me on such short notice."

"Hurnh," he muttered.

"I'm here to represent the interests of the Paranormal Police Department in the matter of case 4576-B. We're requesting a warrant for records held in The Zoo pertaining to the arrival and processing of Bethany Black....uh me. We have cause to believe that the contents of those records could shed light on a case and generate further findings for this court to consider."

The judge just looked at me with half-closed eyes. I glanced over at the guard who just shrugged.

"The request has been cleared with the New York precinct's process coordinator and, uh, has been signed off by the senior officer in charge." I knew Sarge and Max wouldn't sign it for me, so I'd waited for after-hours to get Officer Wood to do it. "You'll find all the paperwork in order."

I handed the documents to the guard. He placed them on the judge's desk and slid them toward him. He then took a step back.

The judge didn't even look at it. He just kept staring at me and breathing heavily. The guy was creeping me out. I felt like a slab of meat being evaluated for dinner.

I cleared my throat. "The contents of the folder include a justification for warrant execution resources, including cost, personnel, and the possibility of further warrants."

His breathing got heavier as he stared me down. I didn't want to jeopardize the request by tearing into the pervert, so I filled the silence with a line-by-line breakdown of the warrant request forms. By the time I said, "So that's why I used a ballpoint pen for the form instead of a felt-tip," I knew I was out of things to say.

I stood in the silence of the room. The guard cleared his throat and the judge shot up in his chair.

"Your honor?" I asked.

"Who are you?"

I squinted, feeling confused. "Uh…I'm Officer Black, sir. NY PPD."

"Oh, yeah…I already had your warrant approved before you came in."

"Why didn't you say something?"

"You started talking." He shrugged. "I like the sound of your voice. Put me right to sleep. Older you get, harder it is to sleep, you know! Please, feel free to keep arguing your case. I…could use the Z's."

I stopped my temper from ruining my good argument and found enough strength to say, "I believe I'm done, your honor," with my soothingest fucking voice.

He sighed in a disappointed kind of way. "You sure?"

"PPD business to tackle, sir."

"Fine. Approved."

He slammed his hammer down a few times. Best I could tell, he was trying to make enough noise to wake himself up.

"Thank you, your honor."

"Thank you for the REM sleep, officer."

I turned around before I rolled my eyes.

I slapped the warrant down on Director Camp's desk.

"There's your fucking warrant."

Big Johnson cleared his throat from behind me. I'd

busted into Camp's office so fast I'd missed the troll lurking in the corner.

"Now come on, Bitty," he said in admonishment.

"Sorry, Big Johnson," I replied, turning back to Camp. "There's your fucking warrant, *ma'am*."

She browsed the document, nodded and glanced up at me with something resembling a smile.

"Well done. You got the laziest judge this side of, well, just about everywhere. Did he fall asleep?"

"Just take me to the records room," I demanded.

I was done with looking to her for help. If she was going to play Red Tape with me, then she could suffer the wrath of my silence. It wasn't much of a weapon, but it's all I had. The whole situation made me feel like I was back in The Zoo like the old days. She always held the upper hand, and I always had to swallow my pride to make it through the day.

Camp lit up a new cigar. "Big Johnson. Take her to the records room. Make sure she sticks to the Bethany Black files. No cross-referencing."

"Yes, 'm," the troll mumbled as he stepped into the hallway. He kept one hand on the door knob and gestured for me to follow him. I did, but not before shooting Camp a frown.

She just puffed on her cigar, her face disappearing in the smoke.

"You should go easy on the boss," Big Johnson whispered over his shoulder.

I tried to keep up with his long strides.

"Yeah? Why is that?"

"She looks out for us, Bitty."

"She looks *over* us, buddy."

"Sure, that's part of the job. But she doesn't want us to be hurt. You know?"

I sighed. "Some of us don't like that kind of attention, BJ. I just want her to help me find some answers."

"You want easy answers, Bitty," he said. "You're angry with her because she won't give you those, but when you've been on this planet as long as she has, you begin to understand that the easier things are to come by, the less you learn from them."

"So you're saying that's why she's such a pain in the ass? She wants to make things impossible so we'll learn?" I guess the venom in my voice hit home because Big Johnson's shoulder slumped and he sighed. I felt a little bad about that. "Look, I get it. She takes her job seriously. That's cool. I just wasted four hours going to court for something she could have handed over, though."

"Are you sure it was wasted?"

"What's that supposed to mean?"

He shrugged, swung the door open to the records room, and gestured for me to enter.

After a minute of searching, I found my files.

Or should I say, file?

One thin red folder waited for me, crunched between two massive sheaves of documentation for 'Atticus Black' and 'Roger Bearstone'. I slid the folder out and counted two sheets of paper inside.

Big Johnson growled.

"Looks like I didn't matter much around here, after all," I said, angrily. I slapped the papers down on the steel table and studied them.

One document was my half-page admittance form.

Race: *Weretiger (species range: red)*

Age: *~5 yo*

Sex: *F*

Height: *43 in*

Notes: *Custody of child transferred to Counsel of Endangered Species by Order 17-R, without challenge (see accompanying documentation)*

The other page wasn't even about me. It was Mike's admittance form.

Race: *Weretiger (species range: red)*

Age: *~5 yo*

Sex: *M*

Height: *43 in*

Notes: *Custody of child transferred to Counsel of Endangered Species by Order 17-R, without challenge (see accompanying documentation)*

I held my form up for Big Johnson to read. "See what I mean?" His brow furled. "This is the kind of thing that makes a weretiger lose faith."

Big Johnson flipped through the drawer for any files that may have been misplaced, but I knew better. Someone had messed with my records as soon as I walked through that door looking for answers.

I took a deep breath and tried to calm down. I wasn't going to jump to conclusions about who was behind this sabotage of my past, but I wasn't about to let up either.

"Thanks for your help, Big Johnson," I said as I exited the room.

"Where are you going?" the troll called out after me.

"To see an old friend."

CHAPTER 23

When you're one of the last two of your kind, you sense things.

It's hard to explain, but Mike and I shared a bond that went beyond understanding. I'd say it even defied mystical reasoning. The closest I can come to explaining it is that it was like having a Siamese twin, but instead of flesh binding us, magic did the trick.

Cassandra's brownstone was kitty-corner to Mike's apartment complex. I rushed past her residence and felt a shiver go down my spine. I'd have to face the consequences of my run-in with her later. I didn't know what I'd do about it, but I refused to worry. I couldn't get distracted.

My bond with Mike helped me know his mood before I even entered his building's lobby. He wouldn't take my calls, but Max got frequent reports from Mike's private security team. The word was he was in scary bad shape. Who could blame him? The mob had extracted a claw

JOHN P. LOGSDON & BEN ZACKHEIM

from his front right paw and used it to start building the Gobler army.

I wanted to tell him it wasn't his fault. I wanted to tell him my claws were building the army now. I wanted to do anything to give him some comfort.

I knew that wouldn't be possible the moment Mike's doorman glanced up from his laptop and said, "He told me not to let you in, ma'am. I'm sorry." He angled himself in his chair so I couldn't miss the Glock he had secured to his hip.

"What? Why?" The doorman shrugged. The poor guy was caught in Mike's drama. Not a fun place to be. "Are you sure he meant me?"

He unpinned a photograph from his desk board and held it up for me to see. "Bethany Black. Yes, ma'am."

I rolled my eyes and dropped down on the bench across from the front desk. I rubbed my face with my palms and tried to think of what to do next.

"Fine," I said, sitting back against the wall with a heavy sigh. "I'll wait for him, then."

"Suit yourself, but I haven't seen him in days. He's ordering in everything. Food, supplies, everything."

"Has he had any visitors?"

"I'm sorry Ms. Black, I can't share that kind of information."

An idea slipped across my brain. It was a long shot, but it was all I had. "Can you call up to his apartment and tell him something?"

The doorman's lips clenched as he struggled for a way to wiggle out of this mess. He nodded and picked up the corded desk phone. "What's the message?"

"Tell him Mountain Dew," I said.

He waited for me to say more, but realized I was done. Mountain Dew was my message. "Excuse me?"

"Mountain Dew," I repeated.

He sighed and dialed the room number.

"Hello, sir. I have a message here from Bethany Black. No sir. She's not on her way up. Her message is Mountain Dew." A few seconds passed. "Sir? You there? Yes, sir."

The doorman hung up the phone, let out a slight cough and said, "Room 14R," and then buzzed the lobby door open for me.

"Thank you," I said, in my sweetest voice. He waved me off. I felt bad for the guy.

"Hello Mike," I said to my friend, who looked like something the cat dragged in, played with, barfed up, and played with again.

He turned away from me and walked into the dark apartment. His voice slid from the darkness. "It's a low blow, using our code word like that, Bethany."

Mike and I had come up with a code word for times when we needed help but couldn't explain yet. It had started as a joke, but we'd used it during some desperate times at The Zoo. Why Mountain Dew? We'd heard it was the only magic elixir normals had ever produced. It fascinated us. We were both disappointed when Mike came back from his first New York modeling job with ten thousand dollars in his bank account and a hole in his stomach lining from drinking the stuff. We hadn't used the code word since.

"I don't want to talk to you, Bethany," Mike said.

"That's fine. I'll do the talking. May I come in?"

"No."

"Don't be an asshole, Mike. This is important. We can't have this conversation in the fucking hallway."

"We don't have to have a conversation at all."

"I say we do."

"I'm sorry. I wasn't aware you were my fucking boss."

I walked into the apartment and slammed the door behind me. "I'm your friend, dipshit. And, as your friend, I have some important things to talk about."

My eyes adjusted to the dark quickly, allowing me to see the mess all around us. He hadn't cleaned up in weeks.

Mike walked over and stood in his kitchen, his back to me. "You're going to tell me it's not my fault. You're going to try to convince me I'm in danger. You're going to try to make everything better."

Sure, he was right, but I wasn't going to show him that. I took a chance and threw out the only thing that might get through his messed up attitude.

I flicked on a lamp. "The goblins are using my claws, Mike. Not yours."

That did the trick. He turned to face me and his meek expression shifted. He made eye contact, and I held it there. I wouldn't let it go.

Mike knew I was telling the truth. Or he knew I was saying something I believed to be the truth.

He looked around the room, probably checking to be sure Max wasn't hiding somewhere.

"Go on," he said.

An opening! I felt a weight lift from my shoulders. "Thank you."

"You can't…"

He stopped short and sniffed at the air. He walked up to me and took me by the shoulders. He went half tiger before I could pull away. His nose darkened and his face sprouted orange, white and black hairs. His golden eyes shot through mine like lightning.

Then they settled on the necklaces around my neck.

"What is that smell?" he growled.

I pulled away from him, and backed up. He walked toward me. "What smell?" My voice cracked.

He licked his lips and reached a paw-like hand for my neck. "The necklace. It smells so…"

"Mike, you're scaring me!"

But he didn't answer. His transformation was deep enough to make him unable to speak. He began to communicate like a tiger. The low growl he released was not making me feel any better about my visit.

Mike stepped toward me as his transformation slowly crept forward. By the time he reached me, he was on all fours, staring at me like I was prey.

I went full tiger in an instant, meeting him face-to-face. Then, I snarled.

He backed up, tripped and rolled toward the kitchen counter. He was back to full human by the time he'd hit his head on the bar chair.

He ran his fingers through his hair and then over his face. I'd never seen him like this.

I waited for him to collect himself.

Mike stood and held himself upright on the counter.

"Mike…"

"Do you want a drink?" he asked, looking lost.

I should have known from the tone in his voice that something was wrong. Something I couldn't yet grasp.

Something dangerous.

"Sure," I said, after returning to full human myself.

I unsnapped my 6er's holster.

Just in case.

CHAPTER 24

I did what a lot of us do when a loved one is ashamed. I tried to act like nothing happened.

Watching Mike pace the kitchen, struggling to get his head on straight, was a combination of terrifying and heart-breaking.

What had I done?

What was I thinking, showing up with the necklace around my neck?

Whatever power it held was wreaking havoc on my best friend. I felt trapped in the moment, as if any move I made would set off a bomb.

My presence there wasn't helping anything. It was making things worse. I went from needing to talk to my old friend, to a strong urge to get the hell away from him before something bad happened.

He growled at the faucet, which I took as a sign that my gut was dead-on correct. "I should go."

"No!" he yelled. He tried to settle down, but I could see the struggle in his face. "No," he whispered. Every muscle was tense as he gritted his teeth and tried to swallow the roar boiling under the surface.

"Mike, I can tell you need to be alone. I was wrong to drop by without telling you."

"I'm fine, Bethany. Just sit down and wait for your fucking drink, will you?"

"I know what it's like, Mike. I can tell when you're fighting to stay human. You're trying so hard, it's painful."

He looked at me with more familiar eyes. They were sad, curious, pained, but they were my old friend's kind eyes. "How long have you been fighting it?" he asked.

"A few months now. Since I joined up with the Paranormal Police Department. You?"

He dropped onto a bar chair with a grunt. "Yeah, me too. About that long. What's going on, Bethany?"

I shrugged. I let my guard down like a rookie. He was relaxing, so I relaxed, too. Stupid. "I don't know, Mike. But I'm pretty sure it has something to do with the mess we're in. Like I said, I think my claws are being used to make the army now."

"Why do you say that? Is the army getting bigger?"

I wanted to protect him from the truth. I wanted to spare him the fear. He'd know everything from my expression, so I pushed the words out and hoped for the best. "Yeah, it's getting bigger."

"How big?"

"I can't talk about it too much, Mike."

"Oh, yeah. God forbid you share information with your best friend about something that impacts him directly. Don't be an asshole, Bethany. Tell me what's going on."

"If you're going to be a dick about it, I'm out of here."

He looked meek, hurt. "You've changed," he said. It was meant to be an attack, but it came off like a whine.

"Yeah, I have changed. You've changed, too. That's what happens when you grow up." He stood and pretended to wash a dish. "Look, Mike, I didn't come here to argue. I'm worried about you. You hide away in this apartment all day, alone."

He scrubbed the dish like he wanted to crack it in two. "I'm fine."

"Do you have any modeling jobs lined up?"

He tossed the dish on the rack and snatched up his next victim. "No. It's been slow. That's the way the biz works."

"Bullshit. You always have a way to get a gig."

"Thanks for the vote of confidence, but I think you can lay off now. I get it. Here." He turned and slid a cup across the marble counter to me. I grabbed it, took a sniff, and a sip. It was some smooth whiskey. He took a nip of his own and closed his baggy eyes. He was exhausted. Then again, so was I.

I tried to make eye contact with him, but he focused on his drink.

"Mike, I want to help you."

He smacked the counter with two open palms. "How about backing off then, Bethany? Maybe I just need some time to recover from being snagged off the street like a stray and mined for my body parts."

"You lost a claw, and I'm sorry about that. I am. But maybe you should take a second to relax and—"

"You are just a fucking geyser of advice tonight," he seethed. "Maybe you *should* leave."

I studied his face to see if he really meant it.

He did.

I took a swig of the whiskey and set it down on the counter gently.

"Thanks for the drink, Mike. I'm here if you need me. You know my number."

"Yeah. I know your number." He'd said it as if he knew I was up to something.

I had to pass by him to get to the door. I put as much distance between the two of us as I could, but there wasn't much room to maneuver.

All my instincts told me to be careful.

But my brain thought different. It was Mike. He wouldn't hurt me.

Wrong.

He grabbed my neck in a strong grip that showed me he meant business. He slammed me against the wall, reached one hand down my shirt, and used the other one to shove my head toward the floor.

By the time I glanced up at him, both necklaces dangled from his hand. He'd pulled them over my head.

"Give them back, Mike," I stated, adding a small growl.

"You have two now? Where did you get the second one?"

He held it up in one hand and studied it. His eyes glazed over as he took in the scent, but there was something else happening to him.

Mike was feeling the same force pulling at him.

I had to keep my temper down.

I had to remember that Mike was an innocent, no matter what a prick he could be.

"Mike, it's doing something to you." His head snapped and he looked at me as if he'd forgotten I was there. "Can you feel it? Can you, Mike?"

He didn't break his stare at me. He nodded his head slightly, once.

And he looped a necklace over his head, let it drop to his chest and transformed into a tiger faster than I'd ever seen before.

My necklace fell to the floor. I grabbed it right as Mike broke through the window. Head first.

CHAPTER 25

*M*ike's humongous tiger head was legend.

I used to tease him about the size of the long, wide brick of a thing. It pretty much guaranteed he won every single one of our wrestling matches. All he needed to do was slam into any part of my body with his crown and I'd go sliding across the room. He'd roar, turn into a human and laugh like he was crazy.

He wasn't laughing now.

We were only on the fourth floor, so he landed without hurting himself. I jumped through the jagged hole in the window and went full tiger in mid-air. I landed on the sidewalk just in time to see Mike bound across the street with two strides and leap onto Cassandra's wall. He dug his claws into the brick of her brownstone and pulled himself up to the second story ledge, a long and narrow perch that went around the whole exterior.

Out of all the places in New York, why did he have to live right next to Cassandra? And out of all the places in

New York where he could have made his escape, why her building?

I followed as fast as I could, and slammed into Cassandra's wall a little too hard. I scrambled to the second floor where I quickly lost my battle with gravity. A lucky bite of a flagpole spared me the painful tumble. I hung from the pole by my fangs for a few seconds, swinging back and forth like a furry flag, until one of my back paws clenched the thin ledge. Then I pushed myself up and got my paws under me. I couldn't see Mike anywhere, but I could smell him.

After carefully balancing myself on the platform, I turned a corner just in time to spot him leaping onto a fire escape. He scrambled up, zig-zagging his way up the steps. His claws tore at the steel like dozens of blades across a chalkboard.

He made eye contact with me. I'd been a tiger with him as much as I'd been in human form. I knew him well, no matter what skin he wore.

I did not recognize my old friend.

There was something missing in his eyes. A lack of familiarity...or feeling, maybe. Some part of him was no longer there.

I balanced myself and made it to the fire escape in a few seconds. I didn't know how I was going to catch up to him. His headstart was too long, and it felt like he'd done this run before.

I had to make up for lost time.

Instead of zig-zagging up the fire escape steps, I climbed the balconies straight up.

That did the trick.

I spotted Mike jump to the roof of an adjoining building. The ten foot distance was nothing to him. He skidded to a halt and turned his large head to me, growled and ran off full speed.

With a snarl, I sprinted to the edge and didn't need to think about the leap. I landed on the tar and stone roof and headed in the direction Mike ran. The building's roof was covered in skylights that came up at a forty-degree angle, so I couldn't see him behind the the rows of windows. I ran up to the top of one, dug in my claws for balance, and saw his lithe form move swiftly through the night.

Up and down we ran, as we climbed the skylights and then slid down the other side, following the steady heartbeat of the chase.

I didn't know how it would end. I didn't have a plan. What would I do if I caught him? Would I fight him? I'd likely lose. I'd never beaten Mike in a match. Not even close, as a matter of fact.

Would I need to use the 6er?

Mike reached the edge of the roof and turned left, making a mad dash for the next building over. I was about to lose him, so I started jumping from skylight to skylight, bounding up and down while trying to keep an eye on him. I needed to conserve my energy. He'd make some stupid moves. I knew him well enough to see that coming. So I'd have to be able to leverage his stupid.

I reached the edge of the building and looked up just in time to see Mike at the peak of his leap.

He was beautiful.

Seeing him like that made my heart ache for the old

days, when we would escape The Zoo and run free until Bob, Lou, or one of the other Zoo goons showed up to scold us.

My heart went from aching to dropping as I realized how far he'd just jumped.

The gap between roofs was about thirty feet.

I'd never jumped that far before.

But was I willing to let my friend escape when he was acting like a mad cat? Would I let him loose on my new hometown with a powerful relic wrapped around his tiger neck?

I had no choice. I had to try to make the leap.

Knowing I needed a good head of steam, I turned and ran to the other side of the roof.

After one deep breath, I sprinted. I built up speed and tried to shut up the little voice in my head that told me I was about to kill myself.

I had to hit that ledge at full speed and with an unshakeable confidence that I'd make it.

I didn't have either.

My timing was slightly off and my back claws didn't get a good grip on the stone as I pushed off for the leap.

My heart raced as I reached the halfway point of my arc and started to drop straight down.

CHAPTER 26

*I*t was like a moment out of a cartoon. Time stalled as I looked down at the six floor drop below me.

No dumpsters, or flagpoles, or trucks carrying recycled pillows. I had just enough time to think, "I may survive this, but I don't think I will," before the breath in my lungs rocketed from my body.

Something had slammed into me.

I landed on the roof. Well, I scraped across the roof, is more accurate.

I didn't have time to think about what had just happened. Something had just knocked me silly. Whatever it was, it had saved my life. I struggled for air and then my lungs violently filled up with air. My stomach did some serious acrobatics to keep my last meal down.

I shook off the confusion, searching the rooftops for my savior. I tried to walk, but I tripped over my paws with the first few steps so I had to stop.

I couldn't lose Mike.

He was in no condition to be wandering the city alone.

I used my mandatory recovery time to scope out the scene. My nose didn't pick up anything, but my ears caught the slight sound of pebbles grinding against each other. The pace of the sound could have been the gait of a weretiger, but something was off about it. There was a break in the rhythm. It sounded like a hobbling weretiger.

I ran toward the noise. My focus shifted to a stink that floated all around me. It was either a troll or a goblin. Their sweat had a similar odor, both unpleasant as hell. I steeled myself for an attack.

Honestly, I needed help.

"*Max,*" I yelled over the connection.

"*Dammit, Black! I told you to keep the volume down!*"

"*I need help.*"

"*The first step in recovery is admitting your problem. Congratulations.*"

"*Something is wrong with Mike. I visited him and he went nuts. Jumped out of his apartment window and now he's running around the rooftops.*" I left out the necklace part. I needed to know more about it before I started triggering Max's conspiracy brain.

"*Shit. I'll be right there, Black.*"

"*We may need more backup. I'm smelling something nasty.*"

"*Tiger breath is lethal.*"

"*It's a heavy stink. It's either a troll or a lot of goblins, or...*"

I shut up as I spotted movement on the adjacent rooftop.

I thought I'd lost Mike for sure, but there he was, sitting and licking a paw.

My initial relief crashed hard into fear.

I knew that body language.

Mike was hurt.

He hadn't sensed me yet. I crouched low and stayed out of the city lights as best I could. I calmed my heart and breathing and slipped into hunting mode. I knew his ears or nose would pick me up any second, but I'd get as close as I could while I had the element of surprise.

Every step sounded like a storm, but Mike didn't show any sign of hearing me. In fact, his licking was getting more furious. I didn't like the look of his position. He was licking his paw so hard he almost fell over.

Then he did.

He tumbled to his side and his gargantuan head hit the roof with a thud. His lolling tongue scraped across the tar surface as he kept licking to clean the wound even though his tongue was nowhere near his leg.

I smelled his blood. Then I smelled a touch of burning flesh and fur.

He'd been shot.

CHAPTER 27

It took a hop, skip and jump to reach Mike.

The first detail I noticed was my friend's lack of consciousness. His half-open eyes were locked straight ahead, unseeing. His wet breath released in fits and bursts.

And the dart in his ass was the second thing I noticed.

What the hell was going on?

I went full human and pulled the 6er from its snug holster.

The silence betrayed someone's presence. It was too quiet. It was a forced silence that comes from a strained, amateur effort at stealth.

The moment was heavy.

Someone was waiting for me somewhere in the shadows.

"I know you're here," I said, trying to sound more confident than I felt. I held the weapon steady with both hands. If I could convince them I knew where they were hiding, I'd gain an advantage.

"Relax, Officer Black," a familiar voice ordered me.

I rolled my eyes.

"What are you doing here, Cassandra?" I asked as she emerged from behind a water tower.

"I'm just tracking down the weretigers who clawed my brownstone walls like they were scratch posts."

"Bill me. What did you shoot him with?"

She dismissed the question with a shrug, continuing her perfect track record of being a total bitch. "Something gentle. He'll sleep like a kitten for a few hours and wake up refreshed."

"How did you catch up to us?"

"I'm full of surprises, Bethany. My goodness, his head is immense."

She took a step toward Mike. That was the wrong move to make.

I put Cassandra in my sights. "Step away from him."

She stopped short and crossed her arms. "What do you think you're doing, young lady?"

"Don't waste the Mom Voice on me, Cassandra. Tell me what the hell you're doing chasing us with a fucking dart gun?"

"After you tell me why you were carrying a photo of my husband, officer." She said 'officer' like it was a four-letter word. I let the silence between us linger. Cassandra sighed. "I'm trying to help you, but I'm beginning to think that's a mistake."

"It's a huge mistake, because I don't trust you." I gripped the 6er tight. "I said step back."

Her frown was filled with decades of refinement. She'd honed that thing to make powerful people cower before her. But I wasn't prone to her kind of mind games. Her magic was strong. Too bad it was wasted on me.

She stepped back.

I nodded. "I'm happy we understand each other."

"We do, indeed, officer." She crossed her arms as I knelt down and yanked the dart out of Mike's ass.

I held it up for Cassandra. "You're a good shot on top of everything else?" She shrugged. "Let me see the gun." She didn't move. That was all I needed to know. "Who shot him with this?"

Cassandra didn't answer with her voice. In fact, she pursed her lips until they crept into some kind of a smile. Her eyes told me where I should look to spot my answer.

I gripped the 6er and turned, ready to shoot.

"Hello, Bethany," Big Johnson said. The Zoo's janitor raised his massive hands in the air. One of them gripped a dart gun.

I let the 6er drop to my side. "What the hell is going on here?"

Cassandra stepped in front of the troll. "Like I said, we're trying to help you."

"Then why do I feel like I've walked into a trap?"

Cassandra tilted her head. "Because you're a paranoid person, dear."

"Zip it, lady. I don't want to hear another condescending word from your pie hole."

"Bethany," Big Johnson said with his soft voice. It was the same voice he'd used in The Zoo while I was growing up. It was the settle-down-before-you-regret-it voice.

I wasn't having any of it. "Shut it, Big J! Tell me what's going on."

He dropped his hands down to his side. "How can I shut it and tell you what's going at the same—"

"Stop the smart-ass routine. Why are you miraculously here to help me catch Mike?"

"It's not a miracle," Big Johnson mumbled. "I was visiting Cassandra for our Thursday drink and we noticed two large cats pass the windows on the second floor den. We took the lift to her roof for a better view and spotted the two of you doing your dance. It was pretty amazing, actually."

I shot Cassandra a quick glance to see her response to his explanation. It seemed to be the truth and her direct stare didn't do anything to make me mistrust his answer.

My mind shifted to the highest priority. Getting Mike back to safety. I somehow had to get him secured before he woke up and started his game all over again.

I tried to slip the necklace off over his neck but it was wrapped around it too tight. The necklace was like a collar now. I tried to yank it off. If I could break the chain, I'd fix it later.

"Don't do that," Cassandra said in her cutting, mom voice. I ignored her and tugged harder, but the strand didn't give. At all.

That's when it occurred to me that there'd been some desperation in Cassandra's voice.

I turned back to her. "What do you know about the necklace?"

"Nothing," she said, "but pulling on it might wake him up too soon."

I didn't believe her, but that was par for the course. I wasn't about to push the subject. I had other worries.

"*Sue,*" I said over the connection, "*do we have helicopters available?*"

"*Yeah, I got one in my back pocket here, lady,*" the AI shot back.

"*Good to see you still have no class, robot. I need something to lift a large animal off a rooftop.*"

"*You want me to lift yer large animal off yer rooftop? Is this a euphemism? You hittin' on me, Black?*"

"*What the hell are you talking about? Did someone jerk off on your CPU fan again?*"

There was a slight pause. "*We don't have anything to lift a large animal off a rooftop, no. Figure something else out.*"

"*Thanks for your help, jerk.*"

"*Anytime, peon.*"

"Goddess, I hate that computer," I said out loud.

Cassandra stood up straight and spoke to Big J over her shoulder. "We need to take Mike to my place." She turned back to face me. "If you're looking for a secure spot for your friend, then that's our best bet."

"Oh, is it?" I asked in my most suspicious-as-fuck tone of voice. "What makes that a good idea, exactly? Because I fail to see how putting my best friend in your lab would be any help at all."

"I don't need to put Mike in the lab. We can lay him on the couch."

"I don't think that would be a good idea," Big J said. "He's going to wake up angry."

"We can handle him," Cassandra said with a small grin. "Together."

I thought through my options. We might have been able to drag him to Cassandra's building if we found a way to get him to ground level. Sure, we'd be spotted, but the great thing about New York City is that everyone has seen it all before. And if they haven't, then they assume it's a movie shoot.

But there was no way to lift him. An average adult tiger weighs up to 600 pounds, and Mike was on the large size.

Big J stepped up and loomed over us. He gave me a reassuring smile, as usual. I wasn't happy to find him with Cassandra, but it was good to see him topside. I suspected there was more going on than he'd told me, but I'd get to the bottom of that later.

Big Johnson slapped his massive hands and rubbed his palms together. "I can carry Mike. Been doing it for years." He bent down and slid his hands under the tiger's torso. With one loud heave, Mike dangled from the troll's arms, his tongue dangling from the side of his mouth.

I knew Mike was asleep, but he looked dead. In a moment of clarity, I was hit with a wave of determination.

I needed to save Mike.

Not that it was a new feeling. I'd been trying to save him for months from a world that wanted to drain him dry.

The revelation was that now I'd have to save him from himself, too.

CHAPTER 28

*W*alking into Cassandra's domain felt like entering the lion's den.

I didn't like it the last time I'd visited, and I didn't like it as I followed Big J to the living room. He laid Mike down gently on the couch. The large tiger's mass pushed the leather on the couch to its limit.

Big J dropped onto a chair with a heavy, tired sigh.

"Did anyone see us?" he asked.

I sat on the couch with Mike and laid a comforting hand on his chest. "Yeah, when you snagged your hand on his paw. That roar of yours could be heard downtown."

Big J held up a bleeding palm. "Mike's claws are sharper than when he was at The Zoo."

"They'll stay quiet," Cassandra said, pouring brandy into a glass. "We keep to ourselves up here." She took a sip and sat in the seat next to our troll friend.

"Up here in the clouds, you mean? Above the riff-raff?"

She handed Big J a cloth napkin for his wound. "That's

exactly what I mean. Having a pet tiger would be one of the lesser eccentric hobbies for people who live up here."

We were acting like my last visit to her house hadn't ended in disaster. I saw the photo I'd procured from Sir Pickle was already framed and sitting in a prominent place on the fireplace's mantle.

Cassandra noticed me spot the photo. Her brow tightened as if she was trying as hard as she could to keep control. I didn't understand her rage at a photograph, but I wasn't about to get distracted from the task at hand.

"He's not showing any sign of waking up," I said. "Maybe we should call The Vet."

The Vet was The Zoo's doc. She specialized in, well, everything. She had zero social skills, but she could fix you up if you broke in two pieces.

"The Vet only works in the Nether, Bethany. We have our own doctors up here." She knelt beside Mike and lifted his lips up to examine his mouth. She ran her fingers over his gums and sniffed his spit.

"He's hydrated," she said, "but we need to keep him that way. I'll be right back."

She walked quickly from the room and made a beeline for the steps to her lab. I waited a moment before I turned to Big Johnson.

"Why are you here, Big J?"

The troll shrugged. "I don't see how that's your business, kid."

"I just think it's a big fucking coincidence that you're here on the night when you're just about the only solution to getting Mike somewhere safe and sound."

"You swear a lot now. New York is rubbing off on you."

"Really, BJ? You're deflecting?"

The troll rolled his eyes. "Jeez, Bethany, I'm not deflecting. I'm just making an observation. If you want me to talk to you, you're going to have to show a little more restraint, okay?"

I leaned forward and tried to catch his eye. "You followed me."

He nodded. "I did."

"And now you're here visiting Cassandra at the same time I visit Mike. You can see how that would make me suspicious."

He could have taken the wrong path. He could have lied. He could have stayed silent. Big Johnson was a good guy, though. He leaned back in his chair and sighed heavily.

"I was here to make sure the two of you didn't hurt each other."

"Me and Cassandra?" Big Johnson nodded. "Look, I don't like her, but I can take care of myself. The Director sent you to keep an eye on us?" He nodded again. "Why do I feel like everyone knows something I don't?"

"Because they do," Big J said with a smirk.

His big, toothy grin could be charming when I was in the mood, but it was ugly as shit at that moment.

"You want to tell me what that something is?"

He shrugged. "I just clean, kid. The Director asks me to watch out for my friend, Bethany, and I do what she says. Gladly."

"Why wouldn't she send the boys?"

"Bob and Lou? They're on her shit list."

"They're doing great. I'm still alive, aren't I?"

"It's not that, kid. I get the sense that she wants them to report in more often, but they've been kind of MIA."

I felt a surge of pride in my bodyguard buds. The Director was just mad that they weren't spying on me more.

The troll leaned forward, suspicion pasted on his face like a street sign. "You wouldn't know anything about that, would you kid?"

"Nah. You know those goblins, Big J. They're good at their jobs, but they do it their own way."

"You mean they snap and bicker and accidentally get things done?"

I smiled. I remembered why I liked the janitor. Still, it would take me awhile to get over the shock of seeing him with Cassandra, even if it wasn't his fault he was hobnobbing with a top-class knob.

Cassandra entered the room silently. Her companion didn't.

The beast's green and pink flesh was covered in patchy blonde and black hair. One of its eyes was a cat's eye, the other was a goblin's. The poor thing's ears didn't know which way to go, bending and twisting around as the creature bounced on all four legs like a fawn just learning to walk.

"What the hell is that thing?" Big J asked.

My stomach dropped when I realized who I was looking at.

"Jonny," I answered.

CHAPTER 29

"*D*on't worry, he doesn't bite," Cassandra said with a little too much mirth in her voice. Did she think this was funny?

"Hey, Jonny," I said as casually as I could.

He didn't answer. At least not in any way that made sense to me. I'd been expecting a vocal response, but his face told me much more. One look at his eyes and I could tell that he was scared of me. He whined and backed up behind Cassandra. She patted him on the head and he relaxed.

"She won't hurt you, sweetheart. Not while I'm around."

"Of course I won't hurt him."

She looked down her nose at me. "If I'm not mistaken, you and your PPD partner are responsible for Jonny's current state. So you'll excuse me if I don't take you at your word in this one small case, dear." She was right, but that didn't mean I had to like it. "And showing me your fangs won't change that."

I held my hand over my mouth. Another damn unintentional transformation. I needed to keep my temper under control. It was definitely a part of the problem.

The former goblin had been the first gobler, an experiment that launched an army of the beasts on the city. He was no innocent. He'd been a mobgoblin before he'd been taken and experimented on, but no·one deserved what I saw that night.

Cassandra knelt beside Mike and unrolled a leather pouch on the rug. She ran her fingernails over the line of syringes, blades and tools. She pulled out a syringe and made to stick Mike with it.

I grabbed her wrist. "What is that, Cassandra?"

She pulled her hand away. "It will stabilize his heart rate. The most common side effect of the narcotic is palpitations."

I glanced up to Big J and he nodded.

Within seconds of removing the needle from his thigh, Mike's panting settled down. He brought his long tongue back into his mouth and fell into a calmer sleep.

Cassandra stood and gave me another one of her superior glances. She turned so quickly that she snapped her robe like a whip. The soft snap echoed in the silence of the room. Then a deep snore fell from my friend. I could feel him calm down. Our connection told me he was going to be okay.

Was I wrong about Cassandra? Every fiber of my being told me she was not to be trusted, yet she kept stepping up when it counted. And I kept doubting her. Max always told me to trust my instincts—unless he told me something different, of course. Maybe my gut just needed some more practice.

The thought of Max set a fire that I knew I had to put out. ASAP. Why had he requested me as a partner? It made no sense. If it was true, then he'd been using me for something. But what? A punching bag? A bucket for his neuroses? He could have used anyone for that. Graham would gladly absorb his bullshit, and then ask for more.

Cassandra had left the room, so I turned to Big J and whispered, "I'm leaving him here." The troll just nodded once. "I need your help, though."

"Of course, kid. What do you need?" He'd kept his voice down, too.

I pointed at Mike. "Keep an eye on him. Make sure he stays safe."

"What? Like night and day? I have a job to do, Bethany."

"Please, Big Johnson."

"I can't just invite myself to stay in Cassandra's home. What reason could I give her?"

"You'll think of something." I smiled at him and went for the front door before he could think of a way to wiggle out.

Yeah, I can be an asshole. And don't think that didn't cross my mind as I tried to assess who was being the bad guy when it came to Cassandra and me. She was the one who was tending to Mike. I was the one manipulating my friends to do my bidding.

It was a long walk to the car.

CHAPTER 30

*B*y the time I spotted Max across the PPD HQ's Main Room, I'd lost my nerve.

His small figure floated above the filing cabinet outside Sarge's office. He was ordering Graham to turn the pages of a report for him.

Could I really have it out with him right there? I tried to map out my options. One, confront him now and have the element of surprise. Two, invite him out for a drink and then hit him with my list of questions faster than his brain could process them.

Then, as if he smelled the burning stench of my brain working through the possibilities, the pixie slowly glanced over his shoulder and locked eyes with me. His flapping wings covered his face, but I could still see a rotoscoped version of his mug.

He knew.

One look at me and he knew it was time to answer for his sins.

It struck me that he'd probably been waiting for this

165

moment for a long time. Me? I'd only had a few hours to process it. I was stepping into the ring against a professional asshole, and I was a 1000:1 underdog.

I shoved my way through a few officers who were unfortunate enough to be in my way as the fire in my chest ignited.

I wasn't thinking.

Again.

I transformed.

Again.

Max turned and crossed his arms and hovered. He didn't budge as everyone around him stepped back like an escaped tiger was walking through their workplace.

"I don't talk to tigers," he stated.

I growled.

"What the hell is going on out here?" Sarge yelled from behind me. I turned to see him struggling to zip up his pants as he walked from the locker room. His gut was too big, so he gave up and marched across the Main Room, red in the face and holding up his pants.

I went full human and found Sarge's finger in my face as I stood upright.

"What do you think yer doin', Black?"

"I didn't mean to—"

"You know what? I don't want to hear it! You two go find an empty room and work it out." He sucked in his gut and got the zipper up. "And clean up the blood. I just deputized the janitor."

He walked off mumbling to himself.

"Welcome back, Sarge!" I yelled after him.

He shot his arm up in the air, flipped me off, and slammed his office door behind him.

"My office," Max mumbled at me, just as I said, "Your office."

Our fellow officers stayed several paces back as we stormed toward the doors to the stairwell. He zipped past my head and disappeared into the darkness of the lower floors. By the time I got to his domain, he was settled in behind his desk, doing his best to show authority.

I wasn't fooled.

He was scared.

I realized maybe it was me with the advantage. He'd been dreading this moment for years. I'd been on fire for hours. I didn't have time to overthink. I just had a question. A question he had no choice but to answer.

"Why did you ask for me to be your partner?"

We let the silence in the room stick. He was soaking it in, clearly trying to figure out how he felt. Whatever the reason for his secrecy and double-crossing, now that he had to face it, he must have been reconciling a load of lies and feelings.

Max sighed like he was relieved. I'd bet my claws he was.

"Because I need you to beat the bad guys."

He waited for me to respond.

"Really? That's it? You think my ego is so big that I'll just say, 'Oh, okay, that makes sense!'?"

He lit up a cigar. It's one of his power moves, meant to convey casual authority. "Actually, yeah."

"It's not that big, Shakespeare. Answer my question."

"Black, if there's one thing I've learned in this life—"

"It's that beating around the bush is a coward's path." That got him. His teeth clenched down on the cigar. "You can tell me now, or you—"

"I promised your mother," he broke in.

That shut me up.

I let my pointing finger drop to my side and juggled a dozen questions as they all raced for my vocal cords at the same time.

"How is that…" I choked. "How did you know…" I stopped, blinking. "Promised her what? That you'd make me your partner?"

"That I'd watch out for you."

My face must have shown my confusion.

Max pushed the cigars across the desk. Why was everyone offering me cigars?

I took one and sat down across from my partner. The one who, apparently, had a million surprises ready for me at all times. Max threw his lighter to me and said, "I was in the Old War. I know, I know. I don't look a day over 100, but I was old enough to be a young soldier. I was a nobody, but I was in the right place at the wrong time, or something like that."

"That's not possible. My mother couldn't have been alive during the war. That would make me…" I realized I'd just been given the answer to Sir Pickle's revelation that I was over 100 years old.

"101."

"But how?"

"I'll get to that, Black. I know it's hard, but just settle down. I've practiced this speech for a very long time. Okay?"

I nodded. I must have looked like someone was trying to break into my house. I was scared. No, I was terrified of what he had to tell me.

He put out the cigar in his ashtray. "I got injured. Shrapnel in the leg. I was kept in bed for weeks with a bad infection. It was magically driven, meaning that standard supernatural quick healing crap didn't work. I couldn't stand being still, so I made a hobby out of listening in on the conversations of other patients."

"Classy."

"You going to give me etiquette tips, or listen?"

"Sorry."

"Yeah, you are. So, one day I heard a conversation between a guy in the bed next to mine. Bullet in the back. He was fine, but the healing spells made him a chatterbox."

"Who was it?"

"Be a detective, Black. Take a guess."

"My father."

"Bingo. He was talking to your mother, who, for her part was trying to shut him the hell up. He was talking about private stuff, but he had zero filter. She could only hope the rest of us in the room were in the same dizzy state. Lucky for her, most of us were. Unlucky for her, I was just fine and dandy...and curious as hell."

"What did they talk about?"

"What did they *not* talk about? Your parents were well-connected people, Black. The weretigers were on the endangered species list. The less of you there were, the more influence you had with the powers-that-be. And they were good at wielding that influence, too. Smart as Einstein, both of them."

Max broke his eye contact with me. He was thinking. He was breaking with his script. He was about to hide something from me, or give me a version that was heavily redacted.

"Don't," I said, simply.

His eye met mine again. He smirked. "Yer gettin' good, Black."

"You can go back to lying to me when you're done."

With a nod, he continued. "Your claws, weretiger claws in general, were all the talk back in the day. It was impossible to tell what was true and what was bullshit, but the rumors were that weretiger claws held great power. Depending on who you asked, they could poison the worlds, or blow everything up, or transform us into coffee beans, or somesuch. Your parents knew the truth, and they had the claws to use as leverage."

He glanced over at me and scrunched his face up.

"You getting all of this, Black? You look like you're about to swallow an egg whole."

"I'm fine," I replied. "Keep going."

"They caught me listening in, and it became a big deal. Top secret this and that. I was greener than you were when you walked through these doors. Unlike you, though, I was smart."

"Nice."

"I wanted to help, too." He looked away and let out a long sigh. "When the war ended, the thirty-two remaining weretigers were hunted down for their claws. I helped them stay one step ahead of the contractors and mobsters who wanted them dead. Your parents and I lobbied to establish The Zoo for the safety of all endangered races. We got the budget and the backing from leadership and your mother put you in their care. She and your father stayed with you." Max swallowed hard. "He died six months into his stay. Obviously, your mom was pretty broken up about it and her health deteriorated, too. She asked me to watch over you. She knew you'd be tough to control." His eyes met mine again. "She was right."

No arguing that. I knew I was headstrong, but it wasn't like my pixie partner gave me much leeway to be anything but obstinate.

"When she died they put you in stasis," he added, sounding distant.

"Why?"

"You were a wanderer," Max explained. "Even at four years old, you were an independent soul. They couldn't risk you falling into the wrong hands. Or that's what they told themselves so they could sleep at night." Suddenly, he bellowed, "What?"

His yell made me flinch. I assumed someone was speaking to him through his connection. He wiped his hands over his face.

"What is it?" I asked.

He stuck the stump of the cigar into his mouth and put on his hat. "Mobgoblin attack at the top of Rockefeller Tower."

CHAPTER 31

The two of us were halfway to the exit when my necklace went nuclear.

The room echoed with the sounds of officers prepping for battle. Back slaps, harnesses buckled taut, weapon checks — all of it made a racket that was both inspiring and terrifying.

Max pushed through the door to the garage steps when a pain shot through my neck. It started at the flesh near my throat, but it travelled down my spine and knocked my feet out from under me.

The pain passed as fast as it had hit me. I opened my eyes to find Max hovering over me. He had an expression on his face that I didn't recognize.

"Black! What the hell are you doing? Holy shit."

His eyes went wide as I smelled something cooking. It smelled delicious. Bacon maybe? Just a little charred.

That's when the pain slapped my brain. I screamed and grabbed for the burn wound. That didn't help. The salt and oils of my hands made the agony double-down. A couple of officers grabbed my arms and held them.

"Doc," Max yelled.

"I don't need a doctor," I hollered back. There was work to do. I could control the pain. I could still help.

"Like hell you don't. Here, take this." My partner flew down to my chest and stood on my breasts. He reached into his pockets. "Open your mouth."

"What the hell are you talking—"

He acted fast. He yanked out a small vial and dropped the contents down my throat. An intense warmth took the place of the pain.

"What did you just force-feed me?"

"Whiskey," he said with a dismissive shrug.

Liar.

The doors to the garage loomed across the room. If I could just make my way there, everyone would know I was fine and lay off.

I sat up and shoved through the looming officers.

"The show's over," I said. "Don't you all have a place to be?"

Shakespeare zipped in front of me and hovered in my face, nose-to-nose. "Sit down, rookie." I swung my hand to swat him away, but he dodged it. "The pain might be gone, but that burn needs to be treated."

One of the nurses ran up to me. Her presence made me realize I'd have to play along. For now. I sat down as she examined my neck.

The nurse tsk-tsked. "Oh dear, that will leave a scar. Second degree burn."

"Where's the doc?" Max asked.

"He's prepping the ward for injuries."

Max gritted his teeth. "Fine. Get her in shape. We need her."

"I'm doing my best, officer," she said as she dabbed my wound.

"Black, what the hell just happened?"

"The necklace burned me." I held it up. It was cool to the touch now.

"Why did it burn you?"

"How would I know, Max?" I gave him a dark look. "*You* should know better than me."

He examined the necklace, his head cocking back and forth. "That was your mother's, right?" I nodded. "Take a deep breath, kid." I frowned and thought about telling him to take a deep fucking breath. "Just do what I say for once!"

I closed my eyes and breathed in as deeply as I could. It was hard. I may not have been feeling much pain, but my body knew it was injured and it was fighting off the urge to go into shock.

Mike.

I don't know why, but I thought about Mike all of a sudden. I opened my eyes.

"What?" Max asked.

"I just thought..." I didn't know how to express the 100% bonafide certainty that Mike was in trouble.

"Black, so help me, if you don't tell me what's going on, I'll—"

"Make my life a living hell? I'm there already thanks, partner. I just thought about Mike. I don't know why."

"Yes, you do."

I met his frown and immediately knew he was right.

Mike was in trouble.

"I have to go," I said, standing up. The nurse fell on her ass. I helped her up as Max landed on my shoulder.

Max shook his head. "You're too close. You'll mess it all up. Besides, I need you at Rockefeller, Black. We'll send someone else."

"He's in trouble, Max. I don't know *how* I know that, but I do. I left him at Cassandra's."

Max shook his head like he was trying to rattle loose this new information. "Why the hell did you do that? You hiding something from me, Black?"

"That's funny, coming from your booze hole!"

"Where to, boss?" Graham asked as he stopped short of running into the nurse, who was still trying to tend to my wound.

"We're talking here, Graham!"

"Sorry, sorry. What's the plan?"

"Kid, I appreciate your enthusiasm. Really. But if you don't shut up, I'm going to put you on latrine duty for a month!"

Graham threw his hands up in surrender to Shakespeare's rage, and backed off a couple of steps. Fay joined Graham by his side, arms crossed. The frown she shot me could only mean she was still pissed at me for hiding the photo of her dad from her.

"Give me the necklace," Max said, holding out his hand.

"I think you know what my answer to that is, partner."

"Do it." I could tell he was serious. I reached behind my neck to unlatch it.

It wouldn't budge.

"Do it, Black!"

"I'm trying! It won't come off."

He sighed and flew behind me. I could feel him trying to get it unhooked. I could also feel how hopeless it was. His little grunts almost made me smile, but I didn't have time to tell any small jokes.

I started to walk away. "We're wasting time. I'll join you at Rockefeller as soon as I drop Mike back here."

Max yelled out. "Lee!"

"Sir!"

"Yer in charge, Lee!" I stopped in my tracks. What was he up to? "Take my unit to the scene at Rockefeller and let me know what you see."

"Yessir!"

Lee and Max's emergency team filed out of the room, as battle-ready as I'd ever seen them. Fay and Graham went to join them. But Max flew in front of them and they stopped in their tracks.

"You two are with us."

"What are you doing, Max?" I asked as I started to run for the garage door.

I pushed the doors open just as Max yelled after me. "Helping clean up your mess, what else?"

The doors closed in his face. I'm pretty sure he didn't hear me mumble, "Helping me clean up *your* mess, you mean."

CHAPTER 32

*M*ax's car was still in the shop, so he took another vehicle.

I wasn't surprised he didn't go with me. He had to avoid the conversation, after all. I had about fifty questions for him, ranging from the promise he'd made my mother, to his involvement with The Zoo, to what my parents were like.

But I had a friend in distress. One look in the rear view mirror and I realized I had two friends in distress.

Fay spotted me looking at her and pretended to enjoy the view out of the car window.

"I'm sorry, Fay," I said. "I didn't know the picture was of your dad. If I did, I would have—"

"Looped me into your plans? That's my problem, BB! Why would you hold onto that information and spring it on a room like this was all a game?"

"I just thought…" I trailed off. "I don't know what I was thinking."

"I can tell you, if you care to hear."

179

"Fine, Fay. What was I thinking?" My tone was more condescending that I'd intended.

"You were thinking you'd be just like your partner."

"What the hell are you talking about?"

"You know what I'm talking about. Pulling a stunt like that is exactly the kind of thing Max would do."

"That's bullshit, Fay. You know we're nothing alike."

She laughed. That hurt. It was a spontaneous thing with no premeditation. She actually thought I *was* like Max Shakespeare, professional jackass.

Graham nodded his head. He could only tell what Fay was saying because he couldn't see my lips, so I knew whose side he was taking.

Big surprise.

I had nothing constructive to say. I knew whatever came out of my mouth would be hurtful. I didn't have friends to spare, so I just shut up.

It was hard to focus as I steered, bribed, and cajoled Junker all the way to Cassandra's apartment. The only sounds Graham and Fay made were shooing away the car's vines. He was in a touchy mood.

Max arrived in his loaner car just as we got out of Junker. He crashed into a curb and slammed into the iron gate around Cassandra's building. The engine spit and hissed steam.

Max wasn't big on seat belts, which made me wonder if I'd just watched the unheroic end of New York's most feared officer.

As I reached the wreck, Max flew from the driver's side window. He did some spitting and hissing of his own.

"Fuckin' thing," he barked as he kicked the loaner car's

roof hard. He held his foot in pain, which sent him spinning in circles in the air.

"You okay?" I asked as he righted himself. I peeked into his car. It was a normal car. No pixie customization.

"How did you even drive that at all?" I asked.

"Barely, is how I fuckin' drove it, rookie."

"Ah, the extremes you'll go to to avoid me sometimes, Shakespeare. Impressive."

I pulled my 6er out and moved toward the front door without another word. It wasn't time for pixie banter. It was time to get Mike out of harm's way for good.

What had I been thinking? Leaving Mike with Cassandra was against every instinct. I vowed to never ignore my best guesses again.

I took position on the right side of the front door, while Graham took the left. Fay stood in front of it, firearm ready. Max floated up to the higher floors. He peeked into a few windows and gave the all-clear sign.

I rang the doorbell and listened for any activity. Silence answered and told us everything we needed to know.

I nodded at Fay. She cast her water spell at the door. It broke off its hinges like it was made of cardboard.

We moved in quick and quiet. We'd become a good team. It was too bad we couldn't get along. I went straight for the reception room where I'd last seen Mike.

It was dark, but there was enough light leaking through the drapes from the street lamps to see the mess all around us. I flicked on the chandelier and marveled at the chaos.

The room had been turned upside down. The huge,

heavy couch Mike had been asleep on was in two pieces in the middle of the room. A floor-standing lamp was embedded in the wall. Whatever had thrown it was powerful.

Big Johnson. Dammit.

"Big Johnson! Mike!"

There was no more time to sneak around.

"Dammit, Black…" Max started, but I shushed him. We stood in silence for a few seconds. Then a small sound came from nearby.

"Was that a cough?" I asked.

Fay nodded. We all went in the same direction, finally agreeing on something.

We stopped at the top of the stairway to Cassandra's lab.

I went first, 6er pointed straight ahead.

I almost slipped on the steps. Graham's flashlight shone on the puddle of blood under my feet.

I leaped down the rest of the way.

As I pushed through the painting that covered the lab's secret entrance, I couldn't help but dread my guess as to what I was about to see.

I was right to be afraid.

CHAPTER 33

*M*ike's naked human form lay limp on the floor.

Big Johnson was twisted into a bundle in a corner. The best I could tell, he was leaning against the brick wall, but I couldn't make sense of his position. Something was wrong with his body.

Very wrong.

Jonny cringed in the corner, whining and coughing lightly, as if he didn't want to make any noise. I made the mistake of walking toward him. He screeched in terror and jumped into the glass case he'd been kept in for weeks.

"It's okay, Jonny," I whispered as I knelt beside Mike and put my hand on his bare back.

Mike was alive.

His warm body eased my clenched gut and let me breathe again. I moved my hand up to the necklace and ran my fingertips over the chain.

"I'll meet the medics at the curb," Max said and he flew from the lab.

"Let's lift him up, guys."

Graham and Fay helped me get Mike to a large leather chair. I covered his naked body. His eyes fluttered open.

"Bethany," he said in a croaking voice. He tried to sit up, but I gently kept him leaning back.

"It's okay, Mike."

He pushed himself back upright. "It's not okay." He slapped my hand away.

"Dammit, Mike. Settle down. You're hurt." He stood up, ready to argue, but the blanket fell to the floor. "And you're naked."

"Bethany, you don't understand." His voice was gravelly. "It's Cassandra."

I tilted my head. "What are you talking about?"

"She's the one behind it all." He looked woozy. "Kidnapping me, taking my claw, building the army of mobster goblins. It's all her."

Fay gasped. She covered her mouth with her hands, eyes wide. Graham made a move to put his hand on her shoulder, but she bolted from the room. Graham ran after her.

I knelt in front of Mike and tugged the blanket back over him. "How do you know this, Mike?"

"I heard her on the phone. She thought I was asleep. She said something about the time being perfect to use the claws."

My brain tried to tie up the loose ends, but first I had to make a mental note that my gut instinct about

Cassandra was right. I felt horrible for Fay. It wasn't her fault her mother was a Class-A fucker. Without hearing another word from Mike, I knew it made sense. She was a powerful player in the PPD and The Zoo. She was an expert in weretigers and seemed to know a lot about what our claws could do. Her helpful behavior had always served her own needs, too—keeping Fay away from my cases, learning more about me and Mike, getting him into her goddam custody.

I felt like such an idiot.

Mike could tell I was struggling with the news. He put his hand on mine. His eyes were dull, as if he was ready to pass out. He obviously had a concussion.

A seed of doubt planted itself.

Had Mike really heard Cassandra talking about some master plan? Or was he hallucinating?

"Mike, you just relax." My tone was meant to be comforting, but it came out as condescending.

"Rockefeller Tower," he said, his eyes focusing again. "You need to go. She ordered an attack there."

Well, that killed all of my doubt. There was no way he could have known about Rockefeller.

"We're on it. Stay put." I stood and made my way to Big J. I could hear his heavy breathing as I got closer, but I still couldn't make out what was wrong with him. He must have sensed me because he stirred and lifted his head.

His face was packed with agony.

I gasped.

His arms crossed his chest like he was giving himself a big bear hug. Except his hands didn't reach around to grab the middle of his back. They laid limp below the elbow of the opposite arm.

"Did my best, BB," he whispered. He shifted his weight and bared his teeth in pain.

"Big Johnson, keep still." But he stood too quickly for me to step in. His dislocated arms dangled at his sides. He breathed heavily. The pace of his inhales got fast.

It was as if he were prepping himself for something.

He slammed his left shoulder into the brick wall and roared. It was loud as hell. But it wasn't nearly enough noise to drown out the snap of his shoulder resetting.

I moved to stop him from doing it to his other arm. He bumped me away with his large chest. "Damn it, Big J!"

He answered me by cracking his other shoulder into the wall. He hissed, swallowing the bellow that wanted to escape.

He swooned from the pain.

"That's better," he mumbled, before he fell onto his butt.

"The medics are on the way," I said.

"Cassandra is tough as hell, Bethany. Don't take her on alone, okay?"

I put a comforting hand on his knee. "Cassandra did this to you?"

He nodded. "Her and some of her goblin cat things. Our boy over there, he drew some serious blood from her, though. She and her beasts got the hell out of here once his claws found her gut. They would have finished me off."

"Was her wound fatal, you think?"

He shrugged. "I hope."

"No," Mike said from behind me. "She'll be in pain, but she'll live. We need to stop messing around and go get her."

"*We're* not doing anything, Mike. The PPD is on it."

He wiped his face in frustration. "Yeah, you guys have done a great job, so far. You need me, Bethany. You need Big J, too. You need all hands on deck, and you know it."

He was right.

My old friend was acting like my old friend again, too, but I had a hard time adjusting to the shift. If the necklace had us in some kind of grip, then it was starting to balance out. Still, his rage was intense.

It was reckless.

Dangerous.

I should know. My equally reckless anger was always ready to spring into the world and mess shit up.

"He's right, kid," Big Johnson said as he pushed himself back to his feet. He shook his hands to get the circulation back, and then clenched them into fists.

We sure could use fists like that in a fight.

I shook my head. "I'm not letting you two go into battle in your condition."

"I agree," Max said from the lab's door. He held something in his hands, but I couldn't make it out.

"You stay out of it," Mike told Max. I cringed. I thought my partner would go nuclear on my friend, but he ignored the jab. "I'm done running," continued Mike. "If you guys didn't notice, I'm kind of in the crosshairs of these fuckers. I can't take a breath in peace."

"We can't let citizens endanger themselves, kid," Max responded.

His voice was softer than usual. He was treating Mike with kid gloves for some reason.

"Then deputize me, pixie. I'm done running." Mike gave him a stern stare. "I'm hunting this bitch down."

CHAPTER 34

*T*he silence in the room felt electric.

For a split second, I thought Max would do it. It had been a whole half hour since he last surprised me. He was overdue for a new curveball in my face.

Instead, my partner made eye contact with me and jerked his head. He wanted to talk to me.

"You stay put," I told Mike over my shoulder as I followed Max out of the lab.

As soon as I got to the door, I glanced back. Jonny had scampered to Mike's side and cowered next to his chair.

I rolled my eyes and ran into a giant mass of a man.

Dick, the PPD medic, stood on the steps outside the secret lab.

"KITTY!"

"Dick, keep it down, dude," his partner, Pat, said with a sigh.

I smiled at Dick. He was simple, but he was a damn talented medic. "Hey, buddy. Do a good job in there, okay?"

He smiled and nodded. Then he slipped past me with grunts.

"You guys are keeping us busy," Pat muttered as her giant partner squeezed through the door. She said it lightly, but it made me feel like shit.

"MAN NAKED!" Dick had clearly seen Mike. The secret door clicked shut, leaving Max and I alone in the dark stairwell.

Max wore that disappointed/frustrated/pissed face I'd grown to hate. Dissafruspissed? New word. I would have smiled at my own cleverness, but Max held up the mysterious thing in his hand.

My stomach belly-flopped into my knees.

It was the photograph of Fay's dad.

"Where the hell did you get this?" he demanded.

I was going to ask him how he knew I had anything to do with the photograph. I spotted some movement at the top of the stairs. Fay was eavesdropping. Poorly. That answered my question.

"Sir Pickle gave it to me," I answered, keeping it simple.

He didn't push it. Max had his own motives with that photograph. I knew that because instead of digging deeper, as he always did, he jumped straight to, "Do you know who this is, rookie?"

"Yeah. Cassandra's husband."

"Cassandra's husband…" He took another look at the photograph. "He's Fay's dad?"

I nodded. I didn't like how he was acting. I mean, I never liked the way he acted, but this was different. Max was stymied, and he wasn't trying to hide that fact.

"What's wrong, Max?"

Max noticed Fay at the top of the stairs and handed me the photograph.

"Keep this safe," he said before he flew off. He hovered next to Fay just long enough to bark, "We're out of here. The Rockefeller fight isn't going well."

I slipped the photo into my shoulder bag and ascended the steps toward my friend. I had no idea what to say to her. She shifted on her feet as I approached, so I knew she was struggling with the same problem.

I opted for uncomfortable honesty. "Even if your mother is behind this, Fay, it's not your fault."

Her eyes widened. She wasn't expecting me to get to the point so fast, maybe. Then her eyes teared up and she took in a deep breath through her nose. "I know that, BB. I was going to say that you don't know what you're talking about, but I guess you do."

I thought she was referring to the fact that my parents were part of this chess match we were playing, but then I realized she couldn't know about that. Hell, I'd just found out. "What do you mean, Fay?"

She shrugged. "We didn't choose to be in this mess. We're fighting our elders' war. It's…it's bullshit!"

Fay never swore, so the word had an extra power behind it. Like magic. It echoed down the stairwell and disappeared into her mother's brick walls. I hoped Cassandra felt that rage in her bones. I hoped she would have a moment of regretting her life. I didn't know what drove her to be a mob boss, but whatever it was, she'd lost a lot to get there. She'd lost the most precious treasure of them all.

"Fay, you're right, but we're not going to let them win. Our ancestors, I mean. We won't make the same mistakes. That's how we crawl out of this hole."

The tears were starting to flow. She couldn't get words out, so she nodded once and walked off.

I got ready to fight someone else's fight again. I hoped it would be the last time.

I was going to be disappointed.

CHAPTER 35

We heard the battle before we saw it.

The air cracked from somewhere above us. I couldn't tell if it was magic tearing things to pieces, or gunshots. Probably both.

We were all packed into Junker when we pulled up to the lineup of New York's Finest. The police cars made a rainbow of colors on the tall buildings. It was like a Christmas rave party, without the music. Or the joy.

Max, Fay and Graham got out of the car, but when I tried to open my door, it didn't budge.

"Open the door, Junker," I demanded. When nothing happened, I slid across the front seat and reached for the passenger door. Vines shot from the back and held me down. "What the hell are you doing, you stupid car?"

That's when I spotted my team push their way into the crowd of officers, toward Detective Holmes' tall figure. He loomed over everyone.

It only took about three seconds to figure out what was going on. The car didn't want me to fight this fight.

Yeah, that's not a sentence that should make sense, but it's true.

Junker was worried about me.

I sighed and relaxed.

The vines eased up a little.

"Look, buddy, it's okay. We have a small army of PPD and NYPD out there. The bad guys don't stand a chance." I didn't believe that, and it must have sounded like it. The vines gripped tight again. "Junker, this is my job! How would you like it if I stopped you from rolling around the city like a moving health hazard, huh?" The vines relaxed again. "Yeah, you'd feel like you were in prison. I need to be a part of this team."

I slowly reached for the door handle. He let me grab it, but he clenched down hard when I lifted it. I really didn't want to cut my way out of there. I closed my eyes. "You sense something, don't you?"

Junker let out a soft sound from his heat vents. It was like the rumbling spawn of a cat purr and a soft fart.

"Look, I don't speak Gas-ese, so you're going to have to find a way to tell me what's going on, or I'm cutting my way out of here with my shiny claws."

I went half tiger to show him I meant business.

Suddenly, the vines pushed and pulled at my body, weaving under my arms and slithering between my knees and cradling the back of my head. The driver window squeaked as it rolled open. Junker slid me outside. I tried to struggle free, but his grip was too tight.

I'd had enough.

I went full tiger.

I slashed and bit at the vines, but he was too strong.

194

The vines pressed into my fur like a wrestler's grip. My head was inert. Was he going to break my neck? Maybe he wasn't worried about me, after all? Maybe the car had turned on me?

I couldn't move. I didn't stand a chance against the thing. I stopped struggling and opened my eyes.

Junker had me facing up. I had a great view of Rockefeller Tower on my right, and a bank building on my left. …it was a bank building with a human shape hidden in the shadows. I watched as the figure lifted something big and cylindrical onto its shoulder.

A rocket launcher.

I roared.

Junker let go.

CHAPTER 36

The missile spit out with a loud hiss, kicked its rear end up with a roaring pop, and drew a straight line of white fire at my team.

I was helpless.

All I could do was watch.

Or not watch.

I turned away from the area that was about to blow skyhigh and ran at the bank's street windows.

I lowered my head.

There wasn't time to think about glass thickness, or trajectory, or stacked odds. I didn't have time to do much of anything, except hope that the explosion from behind me would break me through that fucking window.

That's when I felt the heat on my ass. Then I felt my body get pushed into the glass.

I never heard a thing.

Honestly, I don't know how I stayed conscious. Surrounded by silence, I watched debris follow me as I slid on the smooth stone floor. I ended up at the rear of the bank where the tellers would have been lined up during business hours.

I called out over the connection, *"Max!"*

No answer.

I shook my head to try and shove the fog out of my brain. It worked well enough. I spotted a fire escape on the right wall. I shoved my way through it and was relieved to find a stairwell. With a series of leaps, I took the steps in bunches of ten and zig-zagged to the roof level. This had been my hasty plan from the second I'd watched a missile roar toward the people I loved. Once I saw the coward in the shadows, taking aim at them, I knew I had to get him. Getting into the bank was the only chance.

I had to catch him and snag his ass in my fangs.

My gut told me the battle at the top of Rockefeller was a diversion. Cassandra was drawing us up there with her goblers while the rest of her team picked us off at ground level. I'd learned to trust my gut. No doubt allowed.

As I slammed into the roof's door, I was hit with a wave of despair at a random thought.

If this was some kind of end game, then Cassandra wouldn't just attack Rockefeller.

She would spread us out across the city.

I landed on the tarred pebble floor and dug my claws in deep.

The goblin's stench smacked me right in the nose, even with the city burning around me. He spotted me just as my eyes landed on his hidey hole. He scrambled backwards, dropping his gear and sprinting toward the bank's fire escape.

My tiger senses switched on. I felt the predator hunger swell inside. My fangs clenched tight as my muscles tensed for another rooftop pursuit.

But it didn't get that far.

The goblin stopped at the edge of the roof, dimly lit from below by the inferno he'd made.

The flame started at his feet. He screeched as it climbed his pants and swirled around him in a violent circle. His cries stopped suddenly, and what was left of him fell to the sidewalk below.

"Rookie," Max's voice shot into my head hard.

"There you are! Is everyone okay, Max?"

"Yeah, thanks to Graham. He took us into the building through a side door."

"About time we had some good luck. The shooter was a goblin, Max."

"Was?"

"I had him. He knew it, too. He made like a candle."

"He offed himself? Shit. This mess is a big move for the mob. Maybe it's their end-game after all."

The battle above me ramped up. Gunshots and screams dropped down and made me grimace. I looked up to see someone shoved over the edge of the skyscraper's roof. They fell to the sidewalk, out of sight. I'll never forget the slapping sound of the impact. I ran to see who it was. I couldn't tell from that distance, but they wore a PPD uniform.

"We have to get up there, Max. I think we're losing."

"I know we're losing. We're retreating to ground level. Sarge's orders. We need to protect the survivors of the explosion

until ambulances arrive. Keep an eye open for the goblers."
There was a pause. "And Black?"

"Yeah?"

"Watch out. Looks like the monsters are smart as hell now."

A stream of PPD officers ran from Rockefeller Center's wide bronze doors. They positioned themselves around the edges of the carnage. The bodies were everywhere. Some moved and others were as still as death.

I scrambled down the fire escape and ran from the alley. Fay was in position across the street. I joined her. Without a word, we looked up for any sign of snipers in the windows.

The windows were empty of danger.

Too bad the walls were covered in it.

CHAPTER 37

There were a couple dozen of them, at least.

Their numbers had grown since the church attack.

The new and improved goblers slashed their way down the brick walls of Rockefeller like big bugs. Mike and I could climb up a brick wall for twenty feet, or so, but these things took climbing to a whole new level.

It was tempting to open fire, but the assholes had thought of that. They'd brought insurance. Each of them carried someone in their sharp teeth. Some of the victims struggled. Some of them hung from the goblers' iron jaws, limp as corpses.

The end effect was the same. The PPD held its fire.

I took a quick look around.

The others were tracking the goblers with their handguns. The plan appeared to be for us to wait for the monsters to reach ground level and then open fire. We just had to hope they would drop their flesh-and-bone shields before they attacked.

Unfortunately, they did.

Once the frontline goblers reached the third floor, they dropped their victims in perfect sync. Two dozen PPD and NYPD dropped to the sidewalk.

Fay and I fired, but most officers took a few seconds to get over the horror of the cold-blooded maneuver. The only problem was we didn't have a few seconds. The goblers were too fast. They jumped on everyone with a slow trigger finger.

The ammo slowed them down, but it didn't stop them. Not a single one of my bullseyes were enough to take a gobler out of the fight.

Three of the goblers ran right at me. I emptied my 6er into them. One of them screeched, but he didn't stop. With zero seconds to go full tiger, I crouched and got ready to do my best hand-to-hand.

All three of them veered around me.

I wasn't their target.

One of them snagged Fay and threw her over his shoulder.

"Fay!" I yelled as I transformed.

I ran after them and watched two of the monsters take out a PPD officer who tried to help. The one with Fay over his shoulders smacked her in the back of the head and she went limp.

I roared and jumped.

I missed his back foot by an inch.

He scrambled up a wall and pulled his hostage up ten floors within three seconds. I'd never catch them.

"They got Fay," I said through the connector.

Max's gravelly voice shot back before I could finish my sentence. *"Stay put. Be right there."*

I had a great view of the horrible battle. The PPD were doing okay. The fight had become a hand-to-claw affair. Our werebears were working well together, for once, but one of them was pushed back to a curb where she fell on her big furry ass. The gobler crouched low, ready to attack.

Then he went limp and fell to the street, revealing a floating Max, tiny pistol in tiny hand.

It was the first gobler to go down. They all hissed and turned to Max. He flew my way as a couple of them chased him.

"How did you take him down?" I asked, as he pulled to a stop near my nose.

"I shot him in the ear. He's not dead. I don't know what'll kill these fuckers. His balance is shit now, though."

He was right, the gobler was limping along the curb, trying to keep his balance as he spit and snarled helplessly.

The closest werebear had a clear shot and he took it. He caught up to the gobler, put his head in his massive mouth and chomped it off.

"Didn't need to see that," Max groaned before I could.

The werebear let it drop from his mouth and turned around to knock down the closest raging enemy.

The first of the new-breed gobler had been taken down. It was a moment of hope.

A brief moment.

Again, in perfect sync, the goblers let out a cry. It

wasn't from pain, or rage. There was a tone to it that could only mean one thing. They'd moved onto the next phase of their plan, and all we could do was stand around and wait for it.

"Shit," Max said, barely loud enough to be heard over the terrifying sound.

Just as quickly as it had erupted, their screaming signal died. The silence was eerie, especially in Manhattan. It was as if the city was waiting to see what would happen next.

The clawsteps scratched the pavement and we all looked down at Rockefeller's ice rink. A large figure had made its way to the center.

It was Chester's murderer.

The Bitch looked up at us and growled.

I matched her growl with a nastier one.

"Don't even think about it, rookie," Max said.

I could see her fangs flash in the lights of the city. She had one hell of a smirk. I looked forward to wiping it off her face. Literally. Like off her face and on the pavement, right next to her soldier's detached head.

Dark, yeah, but I was done with the goblers' strike-and-flee methods. I was ready to die to prevent them from escaping again. The mess may have been their endgame, maybe not. Either way, it was definitely mine.

Max yelled after me. "Black! Get back here!"

The Bitch jumped over her soldiers and I ran down the steps to the rink. The next round had started. Gunfire and howls of rage and pain erupted from everywhere. Her gait was weird, like a cross between a tiger-sprint and a kangaroo jump. It was hard to read, and I could tell it was meant to confuse me. I knew I had to catch her mid-air, or I risked getting hammered by a surprise strike.

I stopped short, using my back claws to clench the artificial turf, right as my opponent leaped at me. I crouched and flexed the muscles in my rear legs.

Perfect. She'd land where she thought I'd be. Then I'd strike.

But she didn't land where I would have been.

She landed on my back.

I felt searing pain cross my side as we rolled on the ground.

I was in too deep. I didn't even hear the distant buzz above our heads. My whole world was that fight.

My upper fangs found her forearm's flesh and bit in. It was too bad my bottom fangs dug into my own front paw.

She pulled back, yanking her arm away from me. The sound of her ripping clothes was music to my ears. I'd gouged her deep. Sure, she'd hurt me more, but the momentum was mine. She took a moment to get her bearings, but I knew right where I stood. More importantly, I knew right where she stood.

I ignored the growing roar from the night sky and the pain in my side and jumped on her head, angling my claws into her body in a web of slashing strikes. Her screams and the dripping of her blood on the turf made me hungry.

The sound dropped on our heads like a sonic boom. It was as if a fleet of airplanes were going kamikaze on Rockefeller. I looked up to see dozens of human forms hovering in the air, ten stories high. The fliers circled the night sky. Blue and white flame shot from their rocket packs. The roaring fire got loud enough to make me shut my eyes tight as they descended.

It was no use barking orders, or listening for them either. The sound was everywhere and everything.

CHAPTER 38

The fliers had our attention.

PPD, NYPD, and the goblers waited like an audience in suspense.

A few of the newcomers drew weapons from their chest holsters. They turned in circles, slowly dropping from the night sky.

I was in pain, but I had a clear opening. I could have stuck all of my sharp things deep into the back of the closest flier within two seconds.

My gut told me to wait.

It wasn't until they landed in the bright glow of the plaza that I saw them clearly.

The Hunters were getting in on the action.

The smell of oil should have been a big clue, but my scent for The Bitch's blood had overwhelmed everything.

Several of The Hunters landed in a circle, facing outward, ready to fight.

But fight who?

The Bitch shook her ugly head and glared at me. I turned back to human and pulled my 6er on her.

Gunshots rang out all around me. My fellow officers had turned their attention from the goblers and opened fire. Their ammo bounced off The Hunters' armor like spitballs.

"Hold your fire," I yelled.

I didn't know if The Hunters were there to help, but I knew that pissing them off was a surefire way to grow our losses.

Unfortunately, the distraction gave The Bitch all the time she needed to bolt off. I should have taken her out when I had the chance. Notch off another rookie mistake.

"You heard her! Hold fire!" Max called over the connector.

The Hunters returned fire, just like I knew they would. They didn't strike me as turn-the-other-cheek kind of guys.

I went after Chester's murderer. My officer-brain told me she was a valuable target. Bethany-brain told me to take her ass down.

I tracked The Bitch's path up the rink's steps and guessed she'd use the shadows across the street to hide. The wall ornaments were the perfect climbing stones. I made straight for them.

A heavy tug from a vise-grip squeezed me under the belly. The wound on my side burned hot as it opened up from the pressure.

One of the fliers had me by the short hairs.

I snapped at his arms, but he was positioned too far back on my body. I shifted my weight. My tiger form was a hell of a lot heavier than him, but his mechanical suit whirred into action and countered my squirming with brute force. Painful brute force.

I only had one choice.

I transformed back to human. His grip loosened just enough for me to slip free.

Step one, successful.

Step two, don't die from the fall.

I didn't have a plan for this part.

As the pull of gravity established itself in my lower gut, I saw all nine lives pass in front of my eyes. Then another flier slammed into me.

"Stay put or I break you in two, Black," she hissed in my ear.

I knew that voice. It was the leader. The original Hunter. The one who told me to stay out of her business.

She dropped me on a window ledge and I teetered on the edge. I only kept my balance thanks to a couple of fingernails in the old mortar. I had no room to transform again, and the ledge had no window. The wall behind me was brick.

All I could do was watch the battle rage twenty floors below me.

It wasn't going well.

Max's angry voice broke into my head. *"Where the hell are you, Black?"*

"The Hunters thought they'd give me a view. I don't think they're here to hurt us, Max."

"Oh yeah? Tell that to the fuckers who just took down Sarge!"

Shit.

I would have bet my life The Hunters would massacre the goblers like they had in our last encounter. From the looks of it, I had indeed bet my life. And my team's lives. They'd had a bead on the creeps and I told them to hold their fire.

Max interrupted my dive into a black hole of despair. *"Get over here, dammit. We're getting massacred."*

I didn't like the message, but I hated the desperate tone in his voice even more.

"I'm stuck, partner. About twenty floors up." I waved my arms in case he could spot me.

"Lucky you," Max grumbled. A few seconds later, his voice changed a bit and he added, *"Nice knowing you, kid."*

"Wait, what?" I yelled over the connection and out loud.

Rockefeller Plaza's ice rink played opposites and blossomed into a plume of fire.

CHAPTER 39

*D*ebris slapped against the building a few floors below me.

It was yet another sound I'll never forget. Concrete, glass and metal made a chorus from hell, but it was the low, wet thuds that made me scream.

"Max!"

Nothing.

"Fay! Graham!"

Silence.

"Sue, hook me up with anyone PPD."

"No readings," Sue said.

"No readings. What does 'no readings' mean, Sue?"

"It means I'm not getting comm, vitals...nothing."

"From anyone?"

"Yer the last cat standing, Black."

I glanced around frantically. *"Maybe the connection was broken."*

"Not likely, but tell yerself whatever you want."

"How about you make yourself useful? Get someone with wings to get me down from here."

"Maybe you didn't understand me the first couple of times. There's no one left."

"That's not true," a familiar voice broke in.

"Sir Pickle? Where are you?"

"The moon is beautiful tonight."

I wanted to strangle him.

"Sir Pickle, where the hell are you?"

"I suppose the more direct way to answer your question is, 'Look up, Bethany Black.'"

I craned my head and tried to keep my balance. A silhouette looked back at me from the roof a few stories above. I wished vampires could fly at that moment.

A rope dropped past me and snapped as the end unfurled. It swayed right in front of me.

I started to climb but felt the rope get pulled up fast. I was along for the ride. My friend pulled me over the ledge. I stayed on my back, spread-eagle and tried to collect myself.

"I believe your team is alive," Sir Pickle informed me. "Or some of them are, to be specific."

I struggled to my feet. My side still burned but I didn't have time to worry about it. "What happened? Who set off the bomb?"

"That was not a bomb. That was a power I've not seen before."

"What kind of power?"

He glanced at me and then looked away. "I don't know," he said, lying. "But the force of it has disrupted everything. Radio waves, magnetic forces, even magic. Nothing reads right."

I followed his gaze around the city. "How do you know this?"

He glanced back at me before turning his gaze to the sky scape. "I know."

"Okay, then what do we do now?"

"That's not something I can help with, I'm afraid."

"Don't play the enigmatic vampire bit, Sir Pickle. You need to work with me."

I'd experienced my first taste of Sir Pickle's dark side when I'd intruded on his lab a few days before. I got my second taste that night. If I could have spit it out, I would have. I never wanted to see that expression on his face again.

But I wasn't in a mood to be intimidated.

"Fine," I said. "Go back to your hidey hole and I'll go see which of our friends are still breathing."

I hoped he heard my emphasis on 'our' friends. I ran for the stairwell. Part of me hoped he would follow me. Part of me wanted to go solo. I could get a lot more done without worrying about a team.

No, I didn't really believe that, but it's what I told myself so I didn't lose my shit.

The fact is, I'd never felt more alone.

Maybe Sir Pickle was right. Maybe Max had somehow survived that explosion. Something in me felt more isolated than ever, though. And more alone, too.

I reached for the door to the stairwell.

"I cannot help because my help has never benefitted

anyone but the enemy," Sir Pickle's voice came from beside me.

I pulled the door open and walked away.

"I don't have time for a session right now," I replied. "If you didn't notice there are big things happening. Come with me. Or don't. But stay out of my way."

I left him behind, taking the steps down three at a time. The echoes of two sets of footsteps meant he was joining me.

I let the surge of hope flow over me. I was overdue for some hope.

The Bitch had escaped me again. But I had her scent deep in my memory now. There wasn't a place in the city where she could hide.

The explosion had definitely taken people down. I ran past the bodies of a few goblers and a couple of PPD officers, but the streets weren't as messy as I'd feared. In fact, the plaza was in perfect condition. The ice rink looked exactly like it had a few minutes ago.

"The explosion ignited the gasoline in surrounding cars," Sir Pickle shouted from ahead of me.

I looked for Max, Fay and Graham, but they weren't among the dead or injured.

"Whatever happened here, Max knew it was coming. He told me it was nice working with me right before the explosion."

I'm not sure if Sir Pickle heard me. He'd run to the glass doors to Rockefeller Center, but instead of going through them, he ran his hands over the glass and moved toward the walls of the entranceway. The large overhang made a good spot for people looking to get out of the rain.

And for secret doors, apparently.

Sir Pickle stood near a wall with a fresco on it one second, and the next he stepped through a hole in the same wall.

I had to blink a few times to make sure I wasn't seeing things.

"Come, Bethany Black," Sir Pickle said. "It is time for endings long overdue."

I was too struck by the weight of his words to notice we were being followed.

CHAPTER 40

I followed the long, thin vampire into a long, thin tunnel.

The dim light from a single bulb on the far end of the space was barely enough to make the floor visible.

As I pulled out my 6er, it hit me that Rockefeller was where Sir Pickle had chased Fay's dad years before. It was below those floors where he'd pursued the men who had taken over his lab to examine the claws they tore from me.

I wondered if it was a coincidence. But if there's one thing I'd learned as a PPD officer, it was that coincidence usually meant "keep digging, kid."

I heard a sound from behind me. I pointed my beam back, but nothing was there. I thought of going half tiger so I could use my enhanced senses to make sure.

Instead, I kept going until I reached the bulb. It dangled above a crawl space, about waist-high. I looked into the darkness, trying to adjust my eyes so I could see what waited for me in there.

Sir Pickle's face emerged from the darkness.

I screeched like a little girl.

I'm still not sure if it was a smile that crossed his pale face. Better not have been.

"Will you be joining me?" he asked.

"Don't do that!" I snarled.

A long finger crossed over his lips. "Sssshh. We must be as quiet as snowfall as we move forward, Bethany Black."

"Where are we going?"

"It's just a guess on my part, but the flow of this moment compels me. It has pulled me from a drift."

"Sir Pickle. English."

"That is English."

"English with meaning."

"You recall what I told you about my pursuit of the mystery officials who soiled my lab? It was here."

"Yeah, you lost them at a subway stop."

"A subway stop that I was not familiar with. I spent much time trying to rediscover it. After years of failure I realized my mistake was trying to trace my former path through the underground. I started to tap into my network of peers to see if they could provide clarity. Last night, I was told of the hidden door we just utilized."

"Who told you?"

He paused. He was never a guy with a snappy answer, but this was one hell of a long pause. It screamed LIE.

"An old friend," he finally muttered.

"An old friend," I repeated, suspicious. We didn't have time to work on his trust issues. "So we're going to the subway stop?"

"I don't believe it's a simple subway stop, Bethany Black. I believe it's a test."

"A test," I droned, repeating him yet again.

"If you want me to speak plainly, this is where I must abandon the attempt. For you to understand it, you must see it." I must have hesitated, because his face hardened. "Do you trust me, Bethany Black?"

"More than I probably should."

"Come. If my newfound clarity is accurate, I believe this battle is both a distraction and a rallying cry for something completely different. Let's find your friends."

As quickly as he'd popped into my vision from the crawl space, he faded back to pitch blackness. I harnessed the 6er, clicked on my pen light and clenched it between my teeth. I caught up with the vampire and thought of several inappropriate things to say about his ass. Good thing I had a flashlight in my mouth or I would have ruined the creepy mood.

It wasn't the darkness that made it creepy. Something was off. Every few feet forward felt like a fall, like some center of gravity was yanking us toward it...as if there was no going back.

"Douse the torch, Bethany Black," Sir Pickle whispered.

I clicked the light off and experienced a darkness that was more than a lack of light. It was pure. On top of that, my ears felt like they were full of cotton, which made the silence equally unsettling.

I did a partial transform. Just enough for my cat eyes to see the shape of my friend ahead of me. Those cat ears must have come along for the ride, because I heard a new sound, too.

Something churned below us.

Sir Pickle slowly slid a small door open in the floor. He tried to not make a sound, but I heard a muffled, distant voice emerge from the hole.

Whoever was down there was waiting for us now.

I'd never seen the vampire move like he did at that moment. He slid down through the opening with the grace of a snake lunging from its hiding spot.

The churning noise became a screech.

I pulled myself to the door and dropped through.

I should have looked first.

CHAPTER 41

I fell on Sir Pickle.

We twisted up in a knot of undead and half-tiger limbs.

The floor behind us exploded, the shrapnel peppering our bodies with stone splinters.

"Thank you," Sir Pickle muttered.

I looked up and realized my crappy entrance had shoved him out of the way of a missile of some kind.

The damage to the cement floor was too severe to be a bullet.

I looked around for the shooter and instantly gave up.

The subway station could have been your typical subway station, except for the fact that it didn't have one uptown and one downtown track. It had 18 tracks by my quick count. And each track had a subway train on it. They were powered up. They were ready to go somewhere.

We perched on a narrow walkway overlooking the

impressive sight. I didn't get the chance to get a good look around because the tile column next to us shattered.

I shoved Sir Pickle onto the nearest track and rolled after him. The dust settled on us and made it impossible to see who was shooting at us.

I didn't have to see anything to recognize the taunting voice.

"Bethany, you can't stop it," Cassandra called out from somewhere nearby.

"We're not on a first name basis anymore, Franklin!"

I scanned the area using every sense I had, hoping I could pick out her location. There was just too much ambient noise to triangulate anything. On top of that, the age-old smells that infiltrated the area made it impossible to pick up her scent directly.

"It doesn't have to be this way," Cassandra called again. "You could join us. You and your vampire friend would be valuable allies."

I turned to Sir Pickle and whispered, "Is this the subway station where you lost her husband?"

"They've expanded it, but yes this is it."

"Expanded it? How much did they expand it?"

"The station I remember was two tracks."

"Officer Black," Cassandra bellowed in a sing-song tone.

"We're talking here," I replied to the shout and turned back to Sir Pickle to whisper. "That would take one hell of a rogue operation. You can't just build a damn subway station under Rockefeller Plaza without getting attention."

Then it hit me.

Cassandra and the mobgoblins had been working on this station for years. They had to have been. Over the course of time, the smoothness of the construction would be normalized, managed through magical sound dampeners that blocked those above ground from hearing anything. It was all echoes in here, but I imagined everything above the primary subway was shielded in one fashion or another.

To do all this, though, they would have needed help. Loads of it. I just couldn't think of…

Baudelaire.

Suddenly, the real estate and construction deals that Baudelaire had been doing for decades made more sense. She must have helped Cassandra build everything. She funded it. Kept it quiet. Paid off all the right people.

Sir Pickle probably knew more than I did. "Why do they have dozens of trains down here?"

"As I said before, Bethany Black, I believe the battle above serves many purposes."

"They're distracting us above ground so they can move cargo below ground."

He shrugged in a way that said my words were plausible. "The battle also acts as a signal to begin."

"Begin what?"

"That I do not know. Perhaps it has something to do with…"

He trailed off, looking away.

I grabbed his arm tight. "With what, Sir Pickle?"

"It's just a feeling I have," he replied, without meeting my eyes. "The Old War. Maybe it never ended. Maybe its essence is alive and immortal and awakening from its slumber of peace."

"Officer Black?" Cassandra called out again.

I could suddenly sense she was closer now. In fact, she was almost on top of us.

I signaled to Sir Pickle to bend down and follow me. We crouched low and slipped under the nearest train. I shushed him and went full tiger.

The extra kick of cat senses was always welcome. The world came alive in ways I can't explain. Even with the echoes in the underground lair, I could hear Cassandra's footsteps scraping over the dusty platform. I had to assume she was prepping a spell of some kind.

Fay's mother was full of surprises.

Her footsteps stopped right next to our heads.

She must have sensed I was nearby…or she could hear my panting.

I slunk away from her and ran between trains, keeping my paws soft and light and only stepping on the beams, not the gravel.

I was doing a damn good job of it, too.

But it's tough for a cat to fool a cat. At least that's what we like to think.

I felt a strong tug on my tail.

The tug lifted me from the ground and I was slammed into the side of a train. I fell, just missing the electrified third rail, and got my paws under me. I crouched low in a defensive position.

I smelled her before I saw her perched on the train's roof, glaring down at me.

She was wearing a smirk that did The Bitch justice.

CHAPTER 42

*J*should have guessed she'd stalk me like a coward. If I'd stayed a tiger when we first entered the secret door, I would have smelled her on my ass.

As I jumped onto the roof of the train opposite her, I was hit with that feeling again.

I wanted to be a cat. All the time. Bethany Black was weak. She didn't listen to her intuition like cat did. She couldn't run, smell, see, or feel like cat.

The Bitch's snarl snapped me out of my trance. I crouched low just as she spread her arms wide, claws out, and leaped at me.

She was fast.

Faster than me.

She was savage, too.

But she was nowhere near as savage as me.

Her strike struck gold. I couldn't tell if my ear was gone, or if it found some small piece of fur to hold onto, but I knew it wouldn't stay stuck through the fight.

I didn't care.

My claws—the claws that Sir Pickle had summoned from whatever magic he possessed and given to me—seared the dull glow of the station with a furious white light. I lashed out at anything close to me. I didn't care what, or who, I hit.

I tapped into a fury I'd never felt before.

Chester. She took Chester from me. She stole from my pack. She weakened me and mine. My jaw opened so wide, it hurt. Her arm crossed my tunnel vision and my fangs found meat.

A burn blossomed from my neck, but I was too far gone to worry about it. My back leg bent and gave way as my butt scraped across the iron beam of the subway track. The Bitch was doing some damage, but her arm was mine.

It was as if the anger in my core recharged my body. My grip on her arm tightened. My fangs dug so deep that my gums felt the blood flush from her body.

She tumbled away from me, but I still felt the limb in my mouth. At that moment, I knew I'd won.

She thrashed on the tracks, screeching, clutching at the stump at her shoulder. I let her arm drop from my mouth as I watched her.

Bethany Black would never enjoy that moment.

Cat did.

She was my plaything. She was my amusement. Her agony was satisfying.

"I hope the PPD therapist is still alive," Max said, hovering over my head, "because you are one fucked up kitty, BB."

I didn't feel any joy.

Max was alive. Maybe Fay and Graham and Holmes were alive, too. None of that mattered. I snarled and spat. I was ready to take Max on, too. I wasn't an officer of the PPD anymore.

I just wanted to play with my toy.

The Bitch kicked at the gravel and backed away from me. I walked toward her calmly. I wanted her to feel like Chester had felt. I wanted her to know the end was coming. I wanted her to know I enjoyed her pain.

"Officer Black," Max called after me. "Bethany!"

I kept moving forward, tensing my muscles in anticipation of the kill. I couldn't wait any longer. I needed to see her fear. I *needed* her to know killing Chester had sealed her fate.

She struggled to stand on her two feet.

Too bad her knee touched the third rail.

Her body convulsed and the stench of burnt skin, fuming silk, and crackling bone flooded my senses.

The life left her body, but I wasn't satisfied. I moved closer, my nose almost touching her still form.

The gunshot from behind me broke the trance.

I turned to see Max ducking for cover.

Cassandra stood on a platform overlooking the station. She leaned on the rail like a tourist enjoying the view, flanked by four of her goblers.

There was something off about them. They listed left and right, as if drugged, or injured. My nose picked up the scent of urine, decay, and mold. I realized her guards were all bone.

They were starving.

"I've no hope left for you, Bethany," she said. She

turned to one of her beasts. "Kill them. Start with the tiger."

The goblers leaped from the platform, limbs splayed. The sound coming from their throats sent a chill down my bleeding back. I'd never heard the goblers make it before, but I didn't need to be a zoologist to know they were coming for blood.

And meat, if they could get it.

CHAPTER 43

When I don't chow down on a few thousand calories in human form, my tiger form is ravenous when it takes over.

It sucks, sure, but it also adds a certain spark to my mood. The desperation I feel to finish the business at hand and get some nourishment is great in a pinch.

I knew how dangerous I could be with that hunger screaming in my gut. Which meant I also understood how dangerous these famished creatures were as they sprinted at me, bloodshot eyes wide and wet.

I'll admit, even as a tiger, I felt for them. They were pawns in Cassandra's game. She'd probably kept them hungry for exactly this kind of fight, like the Romans had done to the lions and bears in the fighting arenas.

"Back here," Max yelled from behind me.

I wanted a piece of Cassandra, but my survival instincts overpowered my fading taste for revenge. Chester had received his justice. Now all I had to do was live long enough to enjoy it for him.

I slid behind a column and pressed between two dumpsters, leaning on the cool metal as exhaustion took over.

Without thinking, I turned back to Bethany Black.

I felt dull again. Tired. My faded sense of sight and smell was a prison. I wanted it all back. The strength, the speed...the fury.

"You look like something the cat dragged in," Max said, chortling at his own stupid joke right before he laid down some cover fire.

He must have tagged one because a shriek was followed by the sound of scraping claws on cement. The goblers scrambled into my view, off-balance and scared.

I locked eyes with one.

Desperation and rage crossed his face like a mask, and he jumped at me. I pulled out the 6er and brought it up to fire, but he was too fast. His strong, bony grip hurt like hell around my neck. He opened his mouth and hissed. I brought my hand up to block his fangs and he bit down on the tip of the gun.

I pulled the trigger.

Even with him on top of me, diving for my jugular, I didn't want to kill the gobler. His body went limp and heavy, pinning me down.

I tried to push him off when another gobler landed on his dead comrade. The weight pushed the air out of my lungs. I reached for my next breath, but it eluded me. Panic set in as the new asshole enjoyed my helplessness. There was only one chance to take one shot. I bent my wrist and let my gut tell me when to pull the trigger.

Bullseye.

The bullet went into his ear, snapping his head to the side so violently that he almost fell off me.

Almost.

"Some help here," I called out over the connection to anyone who could hear.

Stars danced around my darkening vision.

I blacked out, but the air found its way back into my lungs, and I bolted upright with a gasp. Fay crouched down next to me and laid down some cover fire before shuffling closer to me. She pushed me back down to the floor. The dead goblers were our cover. Their bodies jerked as bullets hit them instead of us.

"Thanks, Fay," I said, gripping my 6er tight. "What did I miss?"

"Max went after Cassandra. We have them on the run. They're using weapons now." She looked at me and blanched. "Oh no, Bethany. Your ear."

"I'm fine," I replied, but now that I was reminded about the injury, my adrenaline couldn't cover the pain anymore. It started to sting bad.

I peeked over the mound of gobler and saw Graham taking cover behind a steel column. Directly across from his spot, the boys crouched low. Bob and Lou looked terrified until they both spotted me.

They smiled and waved.

I rolled my eyes and pointed to the goblers to remind them that they were being shot at.

It wasn't a great time to talk, but I had to know. "What actually happened, Fay? I thought you were all dead."

"So did we," she replied. "The explosion was more a light show with a gust of wind like I've never..." Her voice trailed off, and she took a couple of shots at the goblers to buy time to collect herself. Hey, we all have our ways of relaxing. "Max kept us together. We didn't know which way was up, but he found us and led us into the building. We followed a Hunter here."

"The Hunters...right." I scanned the area, searching for any sign of them.

"I only saw one."

"Whose side are they on, Fay?"

"Their own, I'm guessing." She fired off another round. "I saw them fighting goblers and PPD officers. The explosion, or whatever it was, scattered them too...except the one we followed. She had it together. Like she was untouched by it all. We would have lost her if Max hadn't flown ahead."

Her. Probably the original Hunter. The one who had told me that my interference with the mob was making things worse. There was something familiar about her. It had been eating at me for days, but I couldn't put my claw on it.

"Where did Max follow Cassandra?" I asked.

"The first train in the line over there."

I took my first long look at the trains. A lot of them were buzzing with activity. Small shapes ran from train car to train car, gesticulating and screeching.

They were up to something.

A dread took hold in my chest.

"I've got to help him," I rasped as I stayed low and eased my way around Fay's small form. "Cover me."

"Are you crazy, BB? There's no way you'll make it all the way across the station."

I laid a hand on her shoulder and smiled "That's the spirit, Fay."

"BB, please. We should wait for backup."

"There is no backup," I stated, keeping my eyes on my destination. "We're it. We're the last line of defense against whatever the hell these jerks are up to."

I realized I was talking about her mother. She sighed and then gritted her teeth. "You'd better run fast, Bethany. I don't feel like losing you."

I nodded.

She nodded back.

I stood quickly and ran for the nearest column.

Everything went to shit.

CHAPTER 44

The trains came to life at the same time.

The sound of screeching metal against metal dominated my senses. I pressed my palms against my ear and my ex-ear.

Eighteen moving trains may be loud, but they also provided a lot of cover. I was a tougher target to hit with the chaos all around me. I jumped onto the tracks and used the space between subway cars to get closer to train number one.

Max's train.

I dropped onto the tracks and found two guns pointed at my gut.

"BB," Bob and Lou yelled in unison.

It all happened so fast I didn't get a chance to do anything. A sniper on the platform above us heard them and took his shot. Bob's shoulder jerked forward from the hit.

I yanked the goblin by the shoulders and dragged him

JOHN P. LOGSDON & BEN ZACKHEIM

between the subway cars. Lou followed us and took pointless shots at the shooter, who was dug in like a tick.

"I'm fine," Bob groaned, clutching at the wound. I pulled his hand off. The exit wound was nasty, but he'd live. That is, if any of us got out of there alive. "Go, BB! Whatever you were doin', it's gotta be more important than nursing me. Lou will lay down some cover for you. Right, Lou?"

"Fuck yeah, I'll lay down some thick fuckin' cover!"

He didn't wait for me to thank him. He just ran from the safe spot, guns blazing, screaming like a really tiny Viking. He ran out of ammo but yanked a second pistol from under his vest.

I could have used a second to grab my breath, but Lou was playing his hand…spastic as it might have been.

I laid down my own cover fire, and I'm pretty sure it was my ricocheting round that hit the sniper. I ducked between the next set of subway cars. One more short trip and I'd reach Max's train, *if* I could catch it. It was picking up speed.

"Max," I called out over the connection, hoping it would be back online.

I'd never been happier to hear his grating voice. *"I got this, kid. I need you on another train."*

There was no chance I'd abandon my partner, so I changed the subject. *"Where are the trains going, Shakespeare?"*

I sprinted to his train and caught the end of the rear car.

"I'm trying to figure that out, rookie. I think they have cargo

to deliver. And, before you ask, I don't know what they're carrying."

I crouched low so the mobgoblins in the train wouldn't see me. I needed to catch my breath, since I got winded easily as Bethany. I would have gone full tiger, but I knew I'd need my weapon for the coming fight. When my lungs caught up, I took one deep breath and pulled the car door open.

A dozen mobgoblins turned their eyes toward me.

One of them was right in front of me.

I jammed my palm into his nose and he fell to the floor with a thud.

"Hi, fellas," I said to everyone else as I opened fire.

They scattered.

I ducked behind a couple of seats and reloaded.

"Are those gunshots yours?" Max asked.

"How sweet. You know the sound of my 6er." I removed the jacket from the unconscious goblin lying next to me.

"Dammit, Black, I told you to take another train!"

"I'm not letting you take on Cassandra alone, partner. Sorry."

I threw the jacket across the aisle. A dozen pistols unloaded into the poor, defenseless garment.

That gave me time to unload on eight of the twelve mobgoblins. Well, I shot at them, to be precise. I missed four of them. That left eight of them standing. No-Ammo Bethany versus eight mobgoblins. It *was* better odds than taking on the gobler beasts, but I didn't like my chances.

I waited for a bullet to find its way into my body somewhere, but one look at the mobgoblins and I knew their heavy trigger fingers had emptied their guns.

One of them reached for his belt and pulled a pistol out. Lucky for me, three of his buddies rushed ahead and got in the line of fire. I planted my left foot and took out the front mobster with a straight kick to the gut. He crumpled to his knees. That's when I bent down and slipped my hands under his armpits, lifting him high enough to block the next goblin in line.

I dropped him and grabbed the outstretched hand of the next guy. With a yank, I pulled him toward me and elbowed him in the nose. Blood flew from his nostrils and covered my face. I slapped at my eyes and cheeks as several strikes found their marks all over my body.

For the second time that night, the breath left me. That was okay, though. My tiger lungs were ready to take over.

My vision sharpened as the colors disappeared. My hearing honed in on the arterial blood of the closest attacker. My stomach yearned for fresh meat.

My nose smelled their fear.

The wide-eyed goblins backed away from me as I went full tiger. I snarled and flexed my claws, scratching the linoleum.

The mobgoblins looked at each other.

They ran.

If I were Bethany, I would have laughed at the sight of them scrambling to get through the train door first. They bumped and squirmed and slapped at each other to get the upper hand.

Instead, I found their actions made me angry.

Their jerky movements and desperation were signs of weakness. That made me hungry, too. The saliva poured over my chin as I stepped toward them, confident I could snag two…maybe three.

The rest of them could wait for dessert.

"Bethany," someone yelled from behind me.

Bethany wasn't my name. Who was Bethany?

When I turned to look at the PPD officer. I barely recognized her as Fay. But I didn't see a friend. I saw an obstacle to my meal. Any obstacle to my meal was also a meal.

The split second of distraction let the goblins get away. I was pissed. I turned on the woman at the other end of the car. The one with the weapon in her hand, pointed at me.

I snarled and crouched low and moved toward her.

"Bethany, it's me! It's Fay. Stop. Stop!"

The woman kept jerking the thing in her hand at me.

It made me mad.

I jumped and ran into a wall of pain.

CHAPTER 45

Something hit me so hard it sent my four hundred pound body flying.

I slid across the train backwards until the back of my neck smacked into a steel pole.

I was covered in frigid water.

It must have acted like a cold shower because Bethany came back. Bethany wasn't an enemy in my head that I had to push away. Bethany was me. I was Bethany Black, weretiger. Both human and tiger.

I was in control again.

For the moment, anyway.

Fay leaned against a door, keeping her balance on the wet floor as the subway car swayed its way around a slight bend in the tracks.

"Fay?" The sound of my own voice felt odd, distant. Like it was someone else speaking. I'd gone back to my human form without trying. So much for feeling like I was in control.

"Are you okay, BB? You acted like you were going to eat my head, so I cast my water spell."

I don't know why I laughed. It wasn't funny. I was *definitely* going to eat her, but the idea of telling Fay that? Ridiculous.

"I'm sorry, Fay," I said as I stood and wrung the water out of my hair. "I was just surprised, is all."

Fay wasn't known for hiding her feelings well, and that moment was no exception. She didn't believe me, and she was clearly freaked out. I couldn't blame her.

I just wanted to find a way to bring her back to me.

"What are you doing here?" I asked.

A goblin started to stir from his deep slumber. Fay kicked him in the head. She always had a surprise or two in store.

"I followed you," she answered. "I wasn't going to let you take on a train of mobgoblins and goblers alone."

I smiled.

Fay and I had our share of problems together, but we'd always been there for each other. I helped her when her mother entered the picture and drove her nuts with her controlling, bitchy ways. I'd helped her find herself. She helped me remember who I was.

"Let's find Max," I said.

I turned to the door and peeked into the next train car. It was empty. From what I could see, the car after that was empty too. It's not like subway cars have a lot of places to hide.

Where were the bad guys?

Fay and I carefully walked through three cars before I spotted some movement in the next one.

We got low and peeked through the window, expecting to see a lineup of armed mobgoblins and slobbering goblers.

Instead, we saw Max pacing back and forth on a row of seats. His arms moved around like he was pissed off. I couldn't see who he was talking to, though. I turned to Fay to ask her if we could switch places so I could see better.

But Fay's pale face told me everything I needed to know.

Max was talking to Cassandra.

Fay stood up straight, took a deep breath, and yanked the hell out of that door handle.

"Fay!"

I reached for her, but pulled back at the last second, recognizing that I didn't really want to stop her. Hell, I wanted to do the same thing she was doing.

If there's one thing I learned from Max, though, it was that you should leave him alone when he's doing something surprising or creepy.

This qualified for both.

"Mother, you're under arrest," Fay growled. She aimed her firearm at Cassandra with a straight arm. She meant business, but her body language made clear she wasn't really thinking like a PPD officer.

She was emotional.

She was dangerous.

"I've got this, Fay," I said, training my newly loaded 6er on Cassandra.

"This is my bust, Officer Black," Fay replied with heat. She never called me Officer Black, unless she was pissed.

"Cassandra Franklin, you're under arrest for..." She stopped. Max and Cassandra waited for her to finish. I was curious which charges she'd throw at her, too. "Lots of things."

Yeah, Fay needed some experience arresting people.

"I have things under control here, Officer Franklin," Max stated with more than a little anger in his voice.

"Do you, sir? It looks to me like your perp is pretty comfortable just sitting there, smiling, just like she's done her whole damn life."

Cassandra sat up straight. "Fay Franklin, you watch your tone with me."

Fay shot her.

She shot her in the shoulder, sure, but she shot her.

I don't think anyone was more surprised than Cassandra. Her mouth moved like she wanted to say something, but no voice came out. Finally, a wail flowed from her lungs like a wave of pain and grief.

I'd wanted to hurt her ever since we found out she was behind all of this. I'd imagined all the ways I could cause her pain. But I don't think there was a single thing that could have hurt her more than what I'd just witnessed.

"What the fuck did you do that for?" Max yelled.

"She went for a weapon," Fay answered in a dark, calm voice. But every word from her mouth sounded like it had a comma after it.

She was just making shit up now.

Fay's weapon was still aimed at her mother.

I gently placed my arm on her wrist and led her hand down to her side. Fay looked at me with wide eyes. They filled up with tears, but no sob came out.

Cassandra let out an odd sound. I think it was a sniff. We all looked over at her. She was back in a seated position, shoulders back, eyes half-mast. The regal pose fit her well. I'd always thought it was an act, but even I was impressed at the poise she demonstrated after being shot.

Until the water started to rise.

I felt the chill on my feet first and then the wetness chilled me to my bones.

"Shit," Max said.

He grabbed me by the non-ear. Whatever flesh I had left hanging there was in his tiny palm. I screamed in pain and followed him. He flew toward the door between subway cars and yanked its handle.

The roaring flood of water was chest-high, even with the door open.

Max yelled back to Fay, "Officer Franklin, follow me! That's an order!"

Fay didn't move.

I thought she was the one casting the water spell, but one look at Cassandra and it was clear she was the caster.

Fay was fighting her mother's magic with a spell of her own. The water level around her was lower. She was somehow countering it. She was buying us time.

The door began to close automatically. I tried to stop it, but some kind of emergency setting must have been triggered. I pressed against the door's motor. Max pulled me by the ear until I fell away from the door and landed on my ass.

"No," I screamed as I stood and pounded on the window to the flooded train. The water was churning hard, kicking up dirt and sending it into whirlpools of murk that made it impossible to see in.

I shot out the window.

...I shouldn't have done that.

A geyser covered us in a spray as strong as a firehose. The force of it slammed us against the door of the next subway car.

We lost our balance and fell from the moving beast.

It was a miracle we weren't split in two under the wheels, but we both sat up from the edge of the tracks and watched the serpent of steel rush away, off into the dim gray of the tunnel.

CHAPTER 46

I'd never felt more alone.

When someone you love dies, you can feel a dark emptiness in you and in the world around you. Maybe you could call that lack of light grief. Or mortality. Or a ghost.

In the subway tunnel, in the silence of our loss, Max and I shared a walk in the guts of the city, both dealing with whatever the hell that emptiness is.

I wanted to talk about it. I wanted to go over everything we'd just seen. I wanted to scream and cry. Instead, I asked Max, "Are you okay?"

"Hmmm? Yeah. I'll live." He buzzed in closer. "You? Yer ear is a mess, kiddo."

"Is it still there?" I reached up to touch it, but thought better of it at the last second. The sweat and dirt on my hand would just make it burn.

"Something's there. It doesn't look like much of an ear, though."

"The station is a ways away, Max. Maybe we should get to the surface."

"I was thinkin' the same thing." He pointed to a ladder to the tunnel ceiling. He zipped ahead to check it out. "It's open. All clear. Watch yer step. Those bars are slippery."

"That's a good way to die after a day like this. Survive the apocalypse and perish on a ladder."

I looked up at him, floating near the hatch. I knew a disaster waited for us on the other side of that door.

There were a thousand questions my partner had to answer, starting with what the hell he was doing chatting with the mastermind of armageddon.

So I smiled at him. I don't know why, but it was what I felt.

Max smiled back.

"What's happening, Max?"

His face slipped back to grumpy mode. He pulled on the latch, and his wings beat faster as he shoved the steel plate open. The sound of sirens and the sight of a fire-lit night sky broke our peace.

"We're about to find out."

My eyes couldn't make sense of anything. The fire from the battle wanted to lick the sky, but something stopped the flame from reaching higher than a few floors. The result was what looked like a snow globe from hell, with Rockefeller Plaza in the middle of it all.

"We need to find Holmes," Max stated. "He'll give us the latest."

I scanned over the crowd of people gathered around ground zero. They were all silhouettes in the light of the fire, but Holmes had to be one of the tall ones. Finally, I settled on the tallest figure.

Max followed me as I ran.

Detective Holmes was on his walkie-talkie, yelling at someone while watching the fire lick the invisible barrier in front of him. When he spotted me in the crowd, his expression changed from terror to fake calm.

"What's the latest?" we asked each other at the same time.

"That's a bad sign," Max noted as he caught up.

I noticed Holmes' shirt was covered in blood. "All I know is that we've got heavy casualties, and our emergency crews can't get past this fucking invisible wall. We've got people dying in there and there's nothing we can do about it."

"Have you tried underground?" I asked. "The mob built a whole subway of their own."

"We have officers down there, yeah, but the wall runs underground, too." He glared at my partner. "What the hell are we up against here, Max? You're holding back on me. I thought we had a deal."

I wasn't going to help Max out of this one. I agreed with the detective. That meant I was waiting for an answer, too.

"Not here," Max replied, before opening up his connector. *"Graham?"*

"Here."

"Yer in charge, kid."

"In charge of who? I don't see any PPD around."

"In charge of whoever will listen to you then! You represent us. Don't bother trying to get past the wall. It's not possible

without a squad of wizards. Just help where you can around the perimeter." He didn't wait for a reply. "*Sue?*"

The PPD AI joined the connection with his usual bad attitude. "*What the hell do you want?*"

"*Give me a head count.*"

Holmes must have known all about our connector system because he went back to assessing the scene. A few seconds passed before Sue responded. "*Hard to say. Whatever force is messin' with the connection is still comin' and goin'. As of now, I see ten vitals, not including you three. Three of them are in the PPD ward and expected to recover. The rest are all alive, but none of them respond to me on the connector.*"

"*Probably because they can't,*" Max hissed.

"*How about Bob, Lou, and Sir Pickle?*" I asked.

"*And Sarge,*" Max added.

"*No response. One of them has an erratic heartbeat. Some kind of trauma.*"

"*That's probably Bob,*" I said. "*He was shot in the shoulder.*"

Graham broke in with that frantic voice of his. "*How about I track down some wizards to help us with the wall, sir?*"

"*You leave that to me and Sue, kid. Do what I told you to do! Yer my eyes on the ground here.*"

I could see Graham's pouty face in my mind's eye. "*Yes, sir.*"

Max turned to me. "Saddle yer horse, rookie. We need a ride."

Junker.

I had to hope my buddy wasn't one of the cars that blew up. I slipped through the crowd with the guys on my heels. My stomach dropped when I didn't see Junker where I'd left him.

Gunshots rang out. The crowd ducked and screamed. It took me a few seconds to realize the sound wasn't from a weapon...unless you consider Junker's exhaust a weapon, which would be totally justified.

The car rammed its way through, and over, some parked police motorcycles. He came to a noisy halt at my feet.

"Sorry about the bikes," I said with a wince to Holmes, who gestured for some officers to back off and let us be.

I waved my hands for Holmes and Max to get in. Max had learned to appreciate Junker. Holmes, on the other hand, took one look in the back seat and said, "Shotgun."

They slipped in next to me. Holmes' almost-seven-foot body did not fit well. Though I didn't mind being smushed against him.

"Thank you, Junker," I said. The car let out a purring growl from its vents. "Now I know you were just trying to warn me about the sniper. Sorry I didn't see that before, buddy." My muscles still ached from the strong grip the car had put on me earlier, but it was better than being dead.

"Who's Junker?" Holmes asked.

"Yer in him," Max said with a smirk.

"Excuse me?"

"He's the car," I explained, shooting Max a shut-up-and-don't-be-a-dick frown.

Holmes looked down at me. He had to bend his head forward to fit in the car. "You talk to your car?"

I shrugged and gave him a sideways glance. "Don't you?"

The vines in the back seat slithered over the head rest

251

and slapped the officer across the ear. Holmes covered himself as I threw the creepy plants off of his shoulders.

"Junker, behave!" I grinned at Holmes. "Don't worry, detective. He's just jealous. Aren't you, Junker?"

The vines crept away.

Holmes sunk down in his seat. "Where are we going?"

"PPD HQ," Max said as the smirk left his face. "We have a puzzle to put together."

CHAPTER 47

*H*Q's Main Room was empty.

Not a single soul weaved through the desks, or worked the phones, or stood by the coffee machine.

I could hear the activity from the hospital ward. Its doors were just past my small living area. There were always injured coming and going. I usually hated the noise because it kept me up at night, but now it was music to my ears. Activity meant they were doing the job of keeping us alive.

"Wow," Holmes breathed as we entered the room through the comic book store front. "Classy place." He ducked. "Nice chandelier."

Max shoved the stuff off of a desk until it was clear. He zipped to Graham's desk and tossed notebooks over his shoulder.

"What are you looking for, Max?" I asked.

"Wrong question."

"Fine. Why were you talking to Cassandra like she was an old friend?"

"I was interrogating her, Black."

"That was a gentle interrogation, Shakespeare."

"I adapt to the situation. She gave me three minutes of alone time while her soldiers waited in the next car for the signal to kill me. I took advantage of the opportunity I was given."

We heard someone enter the room from the ward.

It was Mike.

He looked frail, his arm dangling in a sling. His anger hadn't dimmed down, though. That much was crystal clear.

"Mike, you should be in bed," I admonished in a motherly tone, walking toward him.

"Screw that, Beth. I heard we got our asses kicked. I'm going to help."

"*We* got our asses kicked?" Max asked, his disdain thick enough to cut with a knife. "What do you mean *we*, kid? Yer not PPD."

"I'm going to help. You can't stop me from fighting my own goddamn fight. I'm ready to die, so don't think a grumpy pixie can stop me!"

Max and Mike glared at each other. After a long, awkward moment, Max sighed and relaxed. "Fine, kid. If that's the way you want it, but listen to the rest of the story first and see if you still feel the same way."

"What story?" Mike asked.

I didn't have the patience to explain everything. "Why didn't Cassandra just kill you, Max?"

Mike's face turned red. "Cassandra? Where is she?"

"Quiet, Mike," I barked at the same time Max yelled, "Shut up!"

It was clear that Mike wanted to slap everyone in that room.

Max grunted. "Cassandra and I have a history. I didn't *know* we had a history until tonight, but I'll get to that."

"Who the hell is Cassandra?" Holmes asked.

"Cassandra Franklin," I answered.

Holmes blinked. "The super wealthy Cassandra Franklin? What's she have to do with this mess?"

I jumped in before Max could. "She's the mastermind of it all."

"No, Black," Max said, "she isn't."

That hit me like a slap across the face.

"Bullshit she isn't," Mike hissed.

I put a gentle hand on my friend's shoulder, and he clammed up.

"She was running that whole attack, Max," I pointed out, keeping my voice calm. "Maybe you don't understand the whole picture here because—"

"I understand it fine, Black. Now, all of you sit down and listen. You've got to hear some crappy news right now."

The pixie dropped one of Graham's research notebooks on the cleared desk. Holmes, Mike, and I sat down as Max tore a map of the city off of the Operations wall. He laid it across the desk's surface and opened the notebook.

"None of this is going to make much sense to you, Holmes, so just keep yer questions to yourself."

Holmes waved him off. "I'm used to that."

Max looked up at me. He cleared his throat and stuck a pin into the map.

"Cassandra Franklin is married to a motherfucker who I knew as Rolf DeNahl, aka the One-Balled Fiend."

"I've heard of him," Holmes interrupted. "I thought he was dead, though." Holmes scratched his head. "Wasn't he also known as—"

"Osiris," Max finished for him. "He was a student of another fucker by the name of Keller, who you might remember helped take out half the NY PPD recently. Osiris is the guy who…" He paused, his face flushed red and his breath quickened. I thought he was going to fall, so I reached for him.

"Max, are you—"

He slapped my hand away and stuck another pin in the map.

"Osiris is the fucker who killed my partner," he growled with a level of menace I'd never seen from him. Then, he scanned over us, settling his gaze on me. "He's also the new mob boss."

Nobody replied. Even Mike held his tongue.

Max's connection to the case was much deeper than I'd ever suspected. We waited for him to continue.

"I didn't know about his relationship with Cassandra until I saw the picture of her fuckin' sparkler husband in her den."

"What's a sparkler again?" Holmes asked.

I took this one so Max could get a small break and get his composure back. "A fae who can cast spells off a jewel. The spell destroys the jewel in the casting process. The size of the spell is commensurate with the size and/or quality of the jewel. Bigger is better, no matter what you've heard." I cleared my throat. "This is bad, too, because stepping in as mob boss in the diamond capital of the world is a great way to get your hands on gems and jewels."

"I think he's been planning his move for a long time now," Max said, looking down at the map.

I studied the map, too.

It took half a second to see something I hadn't seen before.

My stomach dropped, and all I could say was, "Oh, shit."

CHAPTER 48

*M*ax and I locked eyes, and he nodded.

My suspicions about Baudelaire's New York City real estate deals had been dead-on.

"So, Bethany said 'Oh, shit' a second ago," Holmes said, looking between Max and me like we were playing tennis. "Wanna let us in on why?"

I turned to Max, ignoring Holmes for a second. "You used Graham's Baudelaire research to put those pins down?"

Max nodded.

I turned to Holmes. "This is in regards to the woman we took out under Central Park. Baudelaire was her name. She'd been building an empire of real estate investments for someone. We didn't know who until now."

"Or why," Max added. He raised his hand as if to say, "Go on."

Holmes leaned over the desk and studied the map. "But we know why now? Enlighten me."

I ran my finger over the pins on the map. Max had stuck a few dozen of them, using Graham's meticulous research from our last case on which properties Baudelaire had bought. Around the edges of Manhattan, the Osiris properties appeared randomly placed. But as the pins moved toward the center of the city, a very clear pattern took shape.

18 lines.

"Oh, shit," Mike and Holmes said together.

All 18 lines converged on Rockefeller Plaza. The plaza's spot on the map looked like a sun spreading 18 rays of light on the city.

"The subway," Holmes said. "You said there was a new subway down there, but the only way for anyone to build their own fucking subway is if they can hide the digging."

"And they can hide the digging if they own the real estate above it."

"Not easily," Mike claimed.

I nodded. "You're right. Not easily. But if you have help in City Hall, and if you run the mob, the job is infinitely easier to cover. You could use a few large building projects on the edge of the city, too, as a front to bring in big rigs, workers."

"Like the amusement park on the pier," I whispered. Max nodded. "If you can drill the tunnels with no city oversight, you could finish fast."

"Fuckin' A," Holmes said.

"But why?" I asked. "Why go through all this trouble to make subway tracks? Why attack Rockefeller Plaza?"

Max studied the map as he spoke. "I don't know why

they chose Rockefeller Plaza, but I think the trains are designed to carry cargo of high value."

Max was leading me somewhere. He offered up his sensei face, which could often be mistaken for his I'm-farting face in certain circumstances. I didn't know where he was leading me, though. It was frustrating. I'd figured a lot out on my own, but I was still the student in my own damn destiny.

"Ask the question again, rookie," Max ordered, "but be more specific."

"Why go through all this trouble to build special trains for special cargo under Rockefeller Plaza?"

Max shook his head. "Try again."

"Do we really have time for this?" I asked.

"Black, I am tired of delivering bad news tonight. You can deliver this part to your own self. Ask again. More specific. Five seconds."

My brain went over more specific questions.

Why build subway trains for cargo under the whole city to Rockefeller Plaza?

"Four."

Why build a bunch of trains and tunnels under Manhattan and attack Rockefeller Plaza?

"Three."

Why have several trains converge under Rockefeller Plaza?
"Two."

Not several trains.

"18 trains," I chirped as everything fell into place in my head. "They built 18 trains. Tigers have 18 claws. 18 trains for 18 tiger claws."

"Oh, shit," Mike said, keeping consistent.

"We're saying that a lot tonight," Holmes muttered.

Max pulled out one of his cigars and snipped off the tip. "Do you remember what I told you earlier, Black?"

"You mean the discussion about you being a soldier in The Old War and putting me in stasis for a few decades because I could think for myself?" I gave him my best duck-face. "No, I don't recall that at all, Shakespeare."

Mike leaned forward, eyes wide. "What are you two talking about? Stasis?"

"I'll explain later, Mike."

"Like hell you—"

"MIKE, NOT NOW!" I'd waited too long for this discussion to be sidetracked by someone else's curiosity. I tore my death glare away and refocused on my partner. "Go, Max."

Max cleared his throat. "In the Old War, word in the trenches was that the Badlands had figured out how to channel demon magic. Your parents knew that the Blood Claw spell could make the claws conduits of equal power."

Mike smacked the table to get my attention. "Wait. Parents? You knew Bethany's parents?"

I put my hand on his. "Mike, don't make me castrate you."

He pulled his hand away and crossed his arms.

Max went on. "Your folks knew they had the key to victory in the pads of their paws. Your mother was a brave woman. She gave up four claws so our best people could make it happen. And they did. The enemy saw the stalemate as clearly as we did. Your mom and those wizards were the secret heroes of the Old War."

Holmes spoke up and proved that he could catch on

with the best of them. "So you think this Osiris guy is going to move beyond cracking jewels open for his magic and start using the claws."

Max took a deep drag on his cigar. "It would be an endless source of power, so yeah."

"A sparkler can't use the claws for magic, though, right?" asked Mike.

"That's right, but the claws can feed the mages so they could continuously repair the jewel that Osiris will use as his power source," I ventured. "That would serve to keep Osiris powered while also ensuring that the mages stay so focused on repairing the jewel that they don't get any grandiose ideas of their own."

Max raised an eyebrow. "You're growing, rookie."

"Thanks." I shook my head. "Do you think Osiris is close to succeeding?"

Max nodded his head. "Yeah, I think he is. Those trains are transporting the claws somewhere."

That didn't sound right. In an instant, something occured to me. Something we missed. "No, they're not," I replied, dully.

I don't know where the confidence came from to contradict him like that. He'd just blown my mind with his revelations, and now I was going to try and one-up him? Was I nuts?

But I knew I was right.

I knew it in my gut.

I realized everyone was staring at me. Well, Max was glaring. Everyone else was staring. I rubbed my face and tried to gather my thoughts.

"The wall is keeping everyone away from the plaza," I

said. "The only people we know of who made it out of the subway were you, me and Fay, but we were on a train. I bet they closed the wall behind us as each train left."

I could see Max catch onto my train of thought immediately. Pun totally intended.

"Yer sayin' they're a step ahead of us, rookie?"

"More than a step. I think the trains have already delivered their cargo. The claws are gathered under the center of New York City, ready for Osiris to charge up so he can keep his jewel polished."

Max grinned and said, "Phrasing."

I sighed at him. "So what do we do now?"

"Plan."

"Plan?"

"We're about to go up against a guy who took down the NY PPD, remember?"

Mike tilted his head. "I thought you said that was Killer."

"Keller," corrected Max, "and it was, but he trained Osiris. Now, Osiris has tiger claws and likely a nice beefy jewel to use for channeling."

"Plus mobgoblins and goblins," I added. I was also going to point out that Cassandra could still be a threat, but then I remembered how that train was filling up with water. It was very likely that both she and Fay had faced their final showdown.

The thought was enough to make me nauseous. Fay had been there for me, even if we hadn't always seen things eye to eye. If nothing else, I could take solace in the fact that she'd finally stood up to her mother.

It didn't help much.

I pushed myself up and stretched. Every fiber of my being was sore. My ear was the most tender of all, but it was doing its best to heal. A couple hours and it'd be good as new…hopefully.

"So, planning?" I said as I released a yawn.

"Yep," answered Max, doing a little stretch of his own. "We'll need weapons, maps, cops, and any other forms of help we can get. Hell, we'll probably even need a wizard or a witch…or both." He rubbed his eyes. "This ain't going to be some little battle, gang. It's going to be a war. We damn near lost the last war, and I *did* lose my partner." Max glanced at me briefly. "Not interested in losing another."

That made me feel good.

Max gave me a lot of shit, and there'd been more than one instance where I would have loved to tie him to a rock and launch him into the deep end of a pool, but we *were* partners. It was like a relationship. One from hell, sure, but it was still family…sort of.

"It's going to take a few days to get everything set," Max announced, heading for the door. "We'll need all hands on deck, too, including Mr. Cucumber."

"Who the hell is that?" asked Mike.

"He's talking about Sir Pickle," I groaned as I followed Max out the door, Holmes and Mike following close behind. "Problem is finding him at this point. Sue said his health stats were still showing he's alive, but he hasn't responded to anyone on the connector."

Technically, we could have Sir Pickle tracked, if we went through the trouble of getting a court order. The problem there was that those were rarely provided unless there was a low health check to prove necessity, or if the person had gone rogue, obviously. Since Sir Pickle's health was solid, according to our A.I., that was a no-go.

That gave me a thought.

"*Sue,*" I called through the connector, "*can you check Fay's health?*"

"*I get no readings at all,*" Sue replied, a moment later. "*Probably dead.*"

It was said with zero emotion, making me want to stick my fist through the ether and somehow punch that damn A.I.

Instead, I just disconnected.

Max was mumbling something to himself.

"What's up, Max?" I asked, attempting to refocus on the room.

"Hmmm?" he said, glancing at me with a frown. "Oh, nothing." He then eyed each of us firmly. "Everyone get a few hours of shuteye. I'll put in calls and get everyone I know in on this. We'll need the help, for sure."

I was about to offer to help, but he raised a finger and pointed at my room.

"Rest, Black. I need you healed and ready to go."

With that, he spun and started flying off toward the entrance to his office.

"We're back on planning soon, people," he called out as he zipped through the air. "You'd better damn well have your wits about you, because you know Osiris and his army of dickheads sure as fuck will!"

CHAPTER 49

*W*e could have stayed up all night.

We got a couple of updates from Graham and Sue on the Rockefeller mess, but there was nothing new. No one could get in or out of the plaza. The NY PPD and NYPD clean-up crews were on the scene, along with dozens of detectives, including Holmes, who left us to relieve one of his buddies.

After I filled in Mike on everything, we sat cross-legged on my bed and threw out theories and ideas that covered the gamut.

We argued, teased and even laughed. It felt like old times, except everything was on the line.

Everything.

We argued about why Osiris and Cassandra would need to deliver the claws by train. Why not just box them up and walk them to their destination? My best theory was that the subway tracks were needed to drive electricity along the third rails to supercharge or guide the Blood Claws attack.

267

Mike was convinced that his claws could be used to counter my claws and cancel out the spell. I told him it was worth looking into. That made his chest puff out.

I hoped Max could find someone to help us with the massive pile of magic questions.

But, in the end, we were left with each others' questions, and that was the end of it. There was nowhere to go, but to sleep.

As I stared at the ceiling, my brain got stuck in a black hole of trying to understand why it took them fourteen years and probably billions of dollars to execute their plan.

Mike's snoring started low and peaked at KISS front-row seat volume. I nudged him onto his side. All that did was make the noise break up into endless loud grunts, with a whistling mess of wet sound at the end.

After a sigh, I turned back to my thoughts, finding comfort in my necklace.

I wrapped my hand around it. When you live with something for a while you get to know its texture. Its angles. The way it makes you feel becomes as much a part of it as its firmness, and its smoothness.

I lifted it up to inspect it closer, but my eye was distracted by a faint light around Mike's neck.

His necklace took on a soft white glow.

I don't know what came over me. I knew the necklaces held great power. Great, unknown power. If I'd been smart, I would have kept my hands to myself. I would have waited for someone wiser than me to tell me what was going on with our necklaces.

But I reached out for it.

As my fingertips touched the whirlpool symbol, the light went out.

The warmth in my necklace faded.

Nothing else happened, which was quite disappointing.

I sighed and resumed my stare at the ceiling, willing sleep to take me over.

One thought kept echoing in my head, though.

It's a trap.

We're being played.

EPILOGUE

"They have no idea," a man said from the shadows.

"You say that with too much confidence," a woman shot back from her own corner of darkness.

"Quiet," Osiris commanded from the dim screen. His voice managed to carry weight, even through the monitor's small speakers. "The plan hasn't changed. Things have played out exactly as we intended."

"There are still too many of them," the woman said. "The PPD must be wiped out."

Osiris smirked. "Twenty officers total. Seven of them are trapped behind the wall."

"Thirteen officers can still ruin everything."

"The only problem we have left is Shakespeare," the man said. "He has the smarts, the connections..." His voice trailed off.

Osiris finished the sentence for him. "And his hatred of me? Is that what you were going to say?"

The room stayed silent.

"I find myself in the odd position of telling the two of you to calm down. You've done well. Don't let doubt sabotage our momentum. Our biggest enemy right now is your doubt. It causes lack of focus."

"So he has signed on?" the woman asked Osiris. "We need him."

"He has, yes. He'll have his peers in the city tomorrow."

"Peers," hissed the woman with disdain. "More like slaves."

"I don't care what they are to him. To us, they're the key. And now they're ours."

The room filled with an excitement that made them all smile.

"Go," Osiris said. The two figures rose from their seats, no doubt glaring at each other through the darkness. "Let's finish what we've started and make it all ours."

~

THE END

~

Thanks for Reading

If you enjoyed this book, would you please leave a review at the site you purchased it from? It doesn't have to be a book report... just a line or two would be fantastic and it would really help us out!

John P. Logsdon
www.JohnPLogsdon.com

John was raised in the MD/VA/DC area. Growing up, John had a steady interest in writing stories, playing music, and tinkering with computers. He spent over 20 years working in the video games industry where he acted as designer, programmer, and producer on many online games. He's now a full-time comedy author focusing on urban fantasy, science fiction, fantasy, Arthurian, and GameLit. His books are racy, crazy, contain adult themes and language, are filled with innuendo, and are loaded with snark. His motto is that he writes stories for mature adults who harbor seriously immature thoughts.

Ben Zackheim
www.BenZackheim.com

Ben's storytelling adventures started as a Production Assistant on the set of the film, A River Runs Through It. After forgetting to bring the crew's walkie talkies, losing Robert Redford's jacket and asking Brad Pitt if he was related to Paul Newman (in front of Paul Newman) he decided that film production didn't "speak" to him. Since no one else on the set would speak to him either he knew he needed to find work that required minimal human contact. Writing fit the bill.

CRIMSON MYTH PRESS

Crimson Myth Press offers more books by this author as well as books from a few other hand-picked authors. From science fiction & fantasy to adventure & mystery, we bring the best stories for adults and kids alike.

www.CrimsonMyth.com

Made in the USA
Columbia, SC
28 May 2024

36274434R00171